# LUCKY'S WOODS

MASSIMO PARADISO

First published in 2024 by Eyes & Teas.

Print ISBN: 978-1-7393941-3-4

Ebook ISBN: 978-1-7393941-2-7

A CIP record for this book is available from the British Library.

*For Enid*

BOOKS BY MASSIMO PARADISO

After Arrival

Lucky's Woods

Two Bodies

# PRELUDE

Carla Vogel looked at the drawings she had just finished. Would they be enough to get the ball rolling? If only her brother was here, then she could tell him straight. But she hadn't seen Max in over ten years. It was originally a joint venture, now mostly Max's doing. But she wasn't angry with him, not in the slightest. She felt stupid for what she had wished for. *Be careful what you wish for.* The fool who said that had no idea about these kinds of wishes. Perhaps someone free from the claws of this community might be able to figure it out, perhaps even end it. Her throat caught fire and she coughed wildly. She brought a tissue up to her mouth and let rip. She inspected the tissue after she recovered. Blood. Clotted and dark as night. Her drawings stared back quietly, offering no help. This will have to do. God help us all.

Max Vogel looked out of the plane's window hoping to finally get a look at Ireland as they came into land, but he was only presented with a cloudy grey sea – the same view he'd been looking at since the flight departed London Gatwick. Thick clumps began to pass across the little oval window and the blinking of the wing tips was stifled to the point of uselessness. A little unease crept into his heart as it always did when the time came to land.

He felt a cool hand squeeze his clammy left and turned to see his wife, Natalie, reaching across the middle seat where their child, Enid, sat sleeping. So much for experiencing her first flight.

Max was glad he'd given in to Nat's insistence on joining him. Although they were primarily here on the morbid business of settling his sister's estate, Nat had taken the week off work and said they should try to treat it as a little break for the three of them. In the few days that had passed after receiving the call telling him his sister Carla had died, he'd discovered he was indeed sad. Both his parents had died before their time, and Carla, while estranged, had been his only sibling - the last tie back to their happy family unit before it all went south after their deaths. That part of his life was now over, but he had all he needed in the two seats next to him.

The plane landed unsurprisingly without incident at Galway Airport and they were swiftly taxied off the runway to a gate. The pilot thanked the passengers in both Irish and English. Not having been to Ireland before, Max suddenly panicked about being that rude Brit who hadn't learned any of the native language before heading abroad.

Again, seeming to sense his constant worries as she always did, Nat gave his hand another squeeze. 'They all speak English. Don't worry.'

After a successful transaction in unbroken English with the car hire company, Max began to feel a bit more comfortable behind the wheel. Driving relaxed him. Since passing his test at the age of seventeen, he'd always been behind the wheel. He swiftly received his taxi licence for bread and butter, then picked up any other jobs that had an office on four wheels. Be it for work or pleasure, he enjoyed the road. The fact Max hadn't spoken to his sister in years meant the idea of weaving in a break didn't leave a bad taste in his mouth. Afterall, it was the first time they had left the country since having their first child. Enid was just fourteen months old now and her independence and thirst for experience was already frightening them both – but they were happy to oblige.

Getting out of Galway proved to be slow going, but as they wiggled their way north west, now under that blanket of grey cloud, Enid awoke wide-eyed and chatty. For some parents, this was hell, but Max always thought it made traffic more manageable – not something he could say about some of his taxi customers. Soon they were out on the N59 with the countryside whizzing by, and at midday they were on the shore of Lough Corrib where they had planned a quick lunch stop.

Max popped Enid in her baby carrier and Nat gathered their supplies, sandwiches and crisps – all the human body needed for nourishment. Relaxing on a felled Alder trunk listening to the softly lapping waves, Max began to get a hint of what might have made his sister move here. He was quick to argue with himself that such things could be found in England too, in places not too far from their home in Furlong, Sussex.

*She's dead and you're still trying to be in the right.*

'It's lovely, isn't it?' Nat said as the cloud started to break overhead reminding the residents of this county that, *yes,* it was indeed summer and the sun was always shining, even if you couldn't see it. Across the Lough, the rays burnt the tips of the tall conifers as they swayed in the breeze like candles on a cake. Songbirds suddenly started a chorus overhead and once again something started to wrap itself around his heart, cooing him with warmth and familiarity, as though he had been to Ireland before, as though he had been *here* before. It felt as if Furlong wasn't that far away, and as Enid plonked stones into the shallow shoreline on her wavering feet, Max's eyes stung a little for his sister. But, as the sun cowered once again, the feeling left as quickly as it had come.

## 2

'Fuck,' said Nat.

'Fuck indeed,' Max agreed.

'Well it's only Ireland,' she said, rooting through the glove box again, which wasn't big enough to require a second rooting. 'We're not in the bloody Himalayas. You'd think there'd be a mobile signal in Ireland.'

'I had no idea the landscape was so gnarly over here. It still thinks we're back in somewhere called Leval, Levallin. No, Levallalin. Wow, that's a lotta Ls.'

'Lililalalal,' Enid said from the back seat, trying to help out.

'Yes, that's the one, boppit,' Max said encouragingly. 'Hard to say isn't it?' They had pulled over on the side of an Irish R road with the rain beating down heavily on the car's roof. Max was tapping away at his mobile's frozen map screen and Nat was fishing around for the map that the rental receptionist had assured them was in the car. The engine of their rental Kia was ticking away quietly while keeping a steady stream of air-conditioned crispness circulating, but a glance down at the petrol gauge reminded Max they only had an eighth of a tank left. He was going to give the rental company an earful when he got back to the airport, but for now, all he could do was switch off the car in case they were still a long way away. It was rental one-o-one to ensure that the car had a full fuel tank, especially when full to full privilege had been paid for. Yes, he hadn't realised until after lunch, but still no one could think they had possibly dumped all that fuel in the little time they had had the frugal little car.

'It's Levalllinree,' Nat said, half her body across the back of the car. 'Ah, ha!' She returned her upper half to the front like a slinky. 'Got it.'

'Oh well done, Nat.'

'Right. Let's see. Can you remember what it's called?'

'You're asking me?' Max said. 'It begins with a C but this phone is completely frozen and I can't go back to that screen,' he said, angrily tapping it.

'Where's the letter then?'

'From the solicitors? Oh yeah, it's in my rucksack,' he said, holding down the phone's power button to force a reset.

'Which is…?'

'It's in the…' He turned to face Nat. 'It's in the boot.'

Nat only responded with a raise of her eyebrows.

'Yup, sure. I'll get it. This is resetting anyway.' Max got out of the car to a chorus of further *lals* and *lils* from Enid. What felt like a much heavier downfall pelted him from the side as he ran back and popped the boot. Its agonisingly slow rise gave little in the way of protection, and Max's eyes wandered north up to the tall rocky hills, the peaks of which were gorging into the low dark cloud.

The boot gave up halfway with a final hydraulic sigh – something else to moan to the hire company about. He cranked it the rest of the way with his left hand and snatched his rucksack with his right, slammed the boot shut and got back into the driver's seat a soggy mess.

'I think it cranked up a notch when you opened the door,' Nat said.

'Yeah, I thought it had gotten heavier.' Max unzipped the front pocket and plucked the letter out. 'You better open it; I'm soaked now.' Nat fished out the sheet with all the details and found the information they needed.

'It's Coillte Ádh,' she said.

'If it begins with a C then that's the one. I think my sister likely moved to the one place where they *don't* speak English.' They both searched around on the map and although the sat nav had found the address at the airport, it wasn't reflected in the physical map. The closest they could find was a place called Coillte which seemed to be in about the same area, and seeing as they had no internet to double check, they could only assume it was the right place.

Max brought the car back to life and they were off again with the wipers on full tilt. In fifteen minutes they were off the R road, and in another ten they were on some country lane which looked to go straight on to Coillte. The asphalt on the road started to break up and soon they were weaving the little Kia around potholes the size of ponds. Then it all gave way to a dirt track that led into a forest. Max stopped the car as they reached the forest edge to read the white signage. Everything they had been past so far had featured Irish words at the top with the English translation at the bottom, which for the most part just looked like a phonetic spelling of the Irish words. But this signage featured only Irish words, but at least it was what they were after: Coillte Ádh. Max turned to Nat with a toothy grin to relish in the mastery of their map reading, but she was looking out and up at the forest.

'I didn't know she lived in a forest.'

'I didn't know anyone lived in forests anymore. Well, I doubt it's all forest. Must just be like the New Forest or something. But the Irish version.'

'Yeah.' Nat moved a little uneasily in her seat. 'I guess I was just picturing some sort of village.'

'Well,' Max said, putting the car into first. 'Let's go find out.'

As they entered the shelter of the forest, the rain changed its timbre from the relentless paradiddle to staccato thuds on the car's roof.

The silence in between these was soon filled with cries from Enid in the back.

## 3

Nat bounced outside the car holding Enid close to her, her cries now diminished to little sobs.

'It's ok. It's ok,' she said.

Neither of them were quite sure what had set Enid off but Max hadn't heard wailing like that from Enid since she'd entered this world – not even after having her skull rearranged to slip through the birth canal and leave the little warm studio flat she'd rented for 41 weeks from dear landlady mother. It had reached a note of acute pain, far beyond a mere moan for attention. Max was going to pull over the car and inspect her properly but Nat had insisted, white-faced, that they drive on until they were clear of the forest. Something deep inside Max had trusted her mother's intuition. The forest hadn't been deep, they had seen the exit just as the entrance disappeared round the bend in the rear view mirror. *Perhaps it was the altitude?*

Max looked around at the welcome scene they were now greeted with, having finally made it to Coillte Ádh.

Nat wasn't wrong to have pictured a village, but it was very small. Perhaps more of a bursting hamlet after a second helping of Sunday roast. The thick cloud that had haunted them since landing in Ireland had been driven away, and of course the rain went with it. They were now faced with a postcard blue sky and – as Irish luck might have it – a rainbow, which floated overhead, fading off over the rocky hilltops to an unseen pot of gold. From the foot of the hill where they pulled over, Max reckoned he could make out nearly every building set against this side of the rising hill. Each was set a little distance away from the other, but they grew closer together the higher they went, where they then became terraced in what must be the town square. A few rather grand buildings were scattered around seeming a little out of place for such a small village. They had the same sandy brick base, but even at this distance Max could make out the modern extensions that had been added – some larger than the original building. They crept out like vines from the main house until they met the boundary of another property. Max wondered how big some of them may have gotten without that hindrance.

'Picturesque, ay?' Max said. He didn't get a reply from Nat so he looked around to check she was still there while he had been lost in thought.

She was bobbing side to side while she stared back at the forest, Enid's puffy eyes looked back to Max.

'I didn't like that one bit,' Nat said.

'The crying? No, it hurt me to hear it.'

'I know. Me too. It wasn't just that though.' Nat cocked her head towards the forest but didn't look at it again.

9

'The forest?' Max asked, now turning to face it. It stood proud at the foot of the hill, no trees straying into the neighbouring field. It had a peculiar uniformity to it. He shrugged. 'It's just a forest.' He followed its boundary east and west but the view was soon chopped off by the rising landscape. 'I think it's the altitude,'

'Yes, it's positively mountainous,' Nat said back.

'Well, it's higher than it is in Sussex, easily,' he said, surveying the landscape. 'Higher than that old hill fort, Cissbury Ring. That barely scrapes two hundred metres. This is at least double that. How did we not see it from the road?'

Nat had stopped listening to Max's monologue and was putting Enid back into the car.

Max looked back up towards the village. He thought it all looked rather charming. He didn't know what else to expect of Ireland. Fields?

'Come on,' Nat said. 'We've still got to find Carla's house and then hopefully get some signal to phone the solicitor for the keys.'

Max had enquired about a hotel with the solicitor but only received a hearty laugh in reply. He'd then suggested a B&B, but those apparently didn't exist either. "If you come to Coillte Ádh, you come to see family," the solicitor had said over the phone. The solicitor had been a little confused as to why Max hadn't wanted to stay at Carla's. Not wanting to go into family feuds with a stranger over the phone, Max said they could stay out of town. The solicitor wasn't having any of it and managed to bend Max's arm into staying at Carla's house, saying it was, "pleasant as a pheasant" – whatever that meant – and had plenty of room for the two of them. Again, not wanting to go into family details, Max hadn't mentioned there would be a little one in tow, but seeing as they had a travel cot, he didn't think it would be a problem, especially as it was technically *his* house now anyway. He admired the view one last time, took a mental snap and then got back into the car and drove up into the village.

# 4

---

After spending the best part of half an hour driving around
the village trying to discern road names and house
numbers, it was clear they had brought some attention to
themselves. The first man they passed by had stopped his
hedge-trimming to watch them go by, with no hint of
coyness. After that, they had stopped to let a man help a
blind woman cross the road, which Max couldn't help but
think took a lot longer than needed, even if she was blind.
Then each time they went down a street they had already
been down, there were new people standing at the gates to
their property watching them go by. Nat mentioned a slight
sense of unease, but the thing was, they were all smiling.
Some even waved, and after a while, Nat and Max started
waving back and giggling. Eventually, they were saved
from their misery when a woman in bright red wellington
boots and a gardening apron stepped into the middle of the
road and raised her arms to stop them. She let her hands
fall to her side and made her way over to Max's window.
He zipped it down to greet her.

'Hello. I'm Max,' he said. 'Carla's—'

'Ah, we all know who you are, Maxy. Don't worry about that,' she cut across. Max hated being called *Maxy* but her lilt would have made a songbird blush. It took the edge off. She gave a warm smile like she was greeting an old friend and moved her eyes across to Nat. 'And this will be your gorgeous bride, so?'

'Yes, hi. I'm Nat. Nice to meet you...?' Nat said, in a well wrapped question.

'Ms Kiely.'

'Oh, the solicitor?' Max said.

*Real smooth, Maxy.*

'Well?' she said, gesturing to her gardening attire like it should be clear enough. 'But I'm much more than my work. Did you have a good trip, so?'

'Yes, it's been fine thank you. Bit of traffic, a bit of rain.'

'Grand. Well you've no need to worry about such things anymore. You'll be anywhere in a minute round here once you know where you're going and you can forget about any more rain,' she said finally.

Just then, Enid went into a little song from the back seat. 'Raaaaain, poorin, snoorin,'

Ms Kiely's eyes shot open in a manner Max found hard to pin. Was it excitement or was it horror? But they returned to their soft gaze as Enid finished her piece.

'Oh, and a little darling is there. You didn't say, Maxy.'

'Well,' he said, looking around to get Nat's take on this, but she was looking in the baby mirror throwing faces to Enid in response. 'I didn't think it was important. She's no bother, really.'

'And why should she be a bother?' Ms Kiely said, making her way to the back window to get a look, tapping on the glass.

'Look at that little face. She's magical.' Max put it down to surprise. After all, why would anyone be afraid of a baby?

'She's called Enid,' Nat said.

'Beautiful. Ah, little natterer is she?' Ms Kiely said, returning to Max's window and flicking his shoulder with her fingertips. 'No stopping her now.'

Max chuckled back politely, but it wasn't forced. Ms Kiely had made him feel right at home. He hoped Carla had felt the same.

*Oh, now you care about how Carla felt.*

Before he could start reprimanding himself further, Ms Kiely cut across his thoughts.

'Right. Well, you lads nearly did it all by yourselves, but a bit of local knowledge never goes amiss around here. We don't have numbers, it's all house *names* round here. Makes it a devil for finding things if you don't know what you're looking for.'

'It is. Seems we managed to wake the town up.'

'Ah yeah, you did that alright. Don't mind this lot, we're a friendly bunch and we all know you now.' Just then, Ms Kiely took a turn from her hospitable self and shouted to the collection of nearby residents and their dogs. 'Go on, you lot. You've had your peek and you can give 'em a chat once they've settled in.' Then, returning to the polite Ms Kiely, she pointed up the hill. 'You see that one with the green roof?'

'Yup,' Max said, quickly trying to suppress giggles from Ms Kiely's outburst to the locals.

'Well, that's David's place. Don't mind him. Your Carla's is the one after that with the eucalyptus in the front. You know what they look like?'

'My father was a ranger.'

'Ah, so he was. Carla put her green fingers down to that. Well, I don't need to explain anymore then.'

'Do you have the key?'

'That's in the door for you, so,' she replied.

'In the door?' Nat asked.

'Didn't Maxy tell you, love? No one comes to Coillte Ádh unless it's for family.' She took her leave and pointed once again up the road as she went, while shouting, 'Key's in the door!'

## 5

Carla had indeed kept a tidy front garden where a short eucalyptus stood in the centre of a smartly bordered lawn, its leaves hanging sadly over the peeling trunk. Max took another look down the hill, now having a better vantage, and managed to take in more of the views. The forest was about as deep as it had felt on the drive through, but it was very wide. So wide in fact that yet again, he lost sight of it behind the rising terrain. He had a feeling that it might circle the entire hill. Perhaps through the centuries, those living here had pushed back the border bit by bit for firewood until modern fuels had come along, and that's where the border had stayed. Over the forest he could just make out the road they had driven in on separating them from the fields. It certainly did look murkier down there under a low belt of cloud. No wonder they hadn't been able to see it rising into the sky. Max made a mental note to admire it next time they popped out. Beyond that, it all faded to grey in the end, but he knew the North Atlantic sat there waiting, and he hoped to get a glimpse of it before they left. He looked up into those postcard skies once more.

*Odd.*

Max turned back to Carla's. It was a lovely little bungalow. Bay windows stood either side of the doorway like sentinels and there were trellis pinned to the spaces between. Jasmine wound its way around the slats in a uniform manner, framing the windows like living green eyebrows. Little flower boxes sat under each window with an assortment of wildflowers enticing pollinators. Max felt a little pang of guilt that these might soon be dead, but he figured the neighbours were already taking care of them – especially Ms Kiely in her Sunday garden best. His eyes landed on the wide front door and the little twinkling of keys that hung out from the lock.

'When you come to Coillte Ádh,' he said, pointing them out to Nat. They made their way up a little sloped path that took them to the front door. Max instinctively turned the key in the lock and was a little surprised when the barrel turned. The villagers had kept the keys in the door, yet had still felt the need to lock it. They entered a hallway which led off to the bayed rooms left and right, and onwards to what looked like the reception area.

His sister had been a bit older at forty-eight, compared to Max's forty, but the place had a sense of belonging to someone much younger than that. Carla always had an eye for style. From the corridor alone, a few pieces of art instantly caught his eye above a beautiful restored mid-century sideboard. The walls were painted a dark green that seemed to breathe light instead of sucking it in.

Growing up, Max had always tried to emulate Carla's carefree rocker look: boots not trainers, tight jeans, band shirts and hair as long as he dared. After that, she had moved onto a more artistic wardrobe full of turtle necks and chinos, but unfortunately, Max didn't have the balls for such things. Now, his primary look was comfort. A nice comfy pair of trainers and some elasticated shorts.

The only thing that perhaps gave the owner's age away sat under the coat rack: a wheelchair with its leather seat cracked from good use. Max was shamefully unsure whether this had been Carla's, or her late wife's, who had been older still. His eyes had rested on the wheelchair perhaps a moment too long as Nat placed her hand on his shoulder and led him on.

They made their way onwards, poking their heads into rooms on the way. Max felt like he was trespassing in not only a property that wasn't *truly* his, but in the life that had lived here too. For years his sister had tried to reconnect, but being bitter as he was, he rode his high, and very weary, horse until his sister had perished. All because he couldn't swallow his pride. Max had never seen it coming to an end like this. He thought in his heart of hearts they would have rekindled their family ties one day. Maybe that was part of the issue. He hadn't seen the rush.

*"You don't know what you've got till it's gone."*
*Thanks Joni.*

The ball had always been in his court, but if he had gone to hit it – no matter how he hit it – he knew Carla would have welcomed him back without any slight on the years of grief he had given her. That pissed him off. She would have been selfless in the act, and no doubt gone on to apologise once again for the hurt *she* had caused – for not being there for him, for not being there for their mum. That was all a bit too easy an out for him to accept.

Perhaps if he knew he'd have needed to fight to win his sister's love back, he would have tried.

Lost in his thoughts, he found his way into an area at the end of the hall, which consisted of a kitchen, diner and living room. The ceiling held a sole exposed wooden beam, which cut across to the rear, where smart bifold doors led onto a garden. Taking in the space, his mind went for a stroll again. Was that the chair she always tried to call him from? Was that the desk where she'd written so many unread letters to him? Once again, his feet were leading him. He sensed that Nat was keeping a close eye on him from behind, with Enid lending a wary pair to this new environment too. He reached the fireplace mantlepiece where a collection of photos were on display. His eyes hopped across them at speed, looking out for the one he knew would be here – and it was, right in the centre. He reached forward and picked up a framed photo from his wedding day. It showed Max in the middle with a smile, already well on the way to drunkenness, his sister on the left looking equally jolly, and on the right was their mother, enjoying the last of her life. Max hadn't noticed the prickling in his eyes, but before long, the tears were steady, and all he wished was that he'd answered an inbound call from Ireland sooner.

# 6

Max never slept well in a new place. Around five a.m. he slipped out of bed, checked Enid, then headed to the kitchen. He let the tap run before finding a glass and filling it with water. The little bungalow was silent and didn't do much talking, which Max liked. Max had been worried he would sense some childish, haunting feeling about the place. But nothing had brought on goosebumps yet. He ambled back down the corridor and went into the bedroom opposite the one they had been sleeping in. It was his sister's room.

The curtains remained open and spilled light into another green landscape. Just like the rest of the house, it was stylishly decorated, but lacked distractions from sleep. A few grayscale prints hung on the wall, inviting visitors to enjoy but not dwell. His stomach twinged at a large cupboard sitting inconspicuously in the corner. That would need emptying. Then there was the bed. It was still made up. Someone had even taken the time to arrange Carla's assortment of pillows – each with a different woodland animal sown in – neatly in place. This is where she had passed away. As he understood it, there had only been a few days of quiet suffering, no drawn out prologue, just the cancer that had been biding its time. He wondered if he would have made the trip over if he had known. Of course he would have.

*Really?*

*Sure.*

He would have come back, if he had answered the phone, but at least there was some relief in the fact her suffering was short.

He smiled to his sister's room and took his leave back towards the kitchen and out into the garden. Ms Kiely's statement rang true and the sky was once again free of clouds. Max felt at the grass with his bare foot and wasn't met with any morning dew so proceeded on. The garden was divided into three sections by overlapping hedges and shrubs so he couldn't see to the end unless he stood dead in the centre. He admired his sister's handiwork in making the garden look so wild, yet clearly it had all been planned out with wise hands. Each section of the garden had a theme. Nearest to the property were evergreens. The middle section was slightly less hardy but got more sun, and right at the back was a forest of flowerbeds ready to bask in another day's warm light. There was a tall wooden gate at the end with all the greenery cut away from the space it needed to function in. It didn't seem to have any locks on it.

'No one comes to Coillte Ádh,' he said to himself as he opened it and poked his head through. There was a little path on the other side which ran parallel to the road, connecting the other gardens sporadically to the path. On the other side of this was a nameless field full of thick gorse and scrub. He nodded in agreement with this layout and thought his sister had had it pretty good in terms of rural setting.

He heard a click of metal to his left and saw a neighbouring gate open, its door swinging out towards him. What had Ms Kiely said about that house? David, was it? He thought about ducking back inside the garden to dodge any awkward conversation, but instead his mind stuck on the fact that he also needed to find out Ms Kiely's first name. He couldn't go on naming her like he was a school pupil the whole time he was here. While he wrestled to get his thoughts in place and make a decision, a man stepped out onto the path and the time to slip away had passed.

The man gave a little grunt in surprise, obviously not expecting to see a strange person in pyjamas standing at the gateway to his dead neighbour's garden this morning, but he seemed to put the pieces together quickly enough. He gave a slow bow of the head and Max caught its meaning.

He returned a smile and the man gave a more perfunctory nod to bring the interaction to an end, closed his gate and headed off down the hill. Max hoped that most of the interactions with the locals would be as swift as that. He struggled with strangers, yet latched onto anyone he felt some connection with. It wasn't a conducive cocktail to making new friends.

## 7

Max didn't know where to start with the clean-up or what manner to do it in. Having now been into all the rooms, and the garage, and poked his head into the attic, it was clear this was going to be a bit of a job, and he found himself wanting little Ms Kiely there to direct him. As if his wish had been granted, there was a knock on the door, and judging by the bright red boots that shone through the lower glass panes, it wasn't hard for Max to guess who it was. He was now dressed in proper clothes, but Nat and Enid were still in their pyjamas taking their breakfast in the garden. Nat could get funny about her attire – pyjamas were strictly for family eyes. He doubted that Ms Kiely was about to bolt straight through to the garden, so opened the door.

He was greeted with a warm smile, another vibrant gardening apron and a loaf of bread which smelt like it had just come out of the oven.

'Good morning. Oh, that's very kind of you,' he said,

taking the bread. It was still warm. 'There was no need for that, we brought plenty of supplies.'

'Ah, stop. I passed by the bakery early. Don't think I went baking it myself,' Ms Kiely said, letting herself in as she had no doubt done a hundred times before.

Still not quite feeling like the owner, Max let her traipse on through in her boots. 'Where's the little one, so?' she asked, a slight look of worry on her face.

'She's just in the garden with my wife,' he replied.

Ms Kiely eased up instantly. 'Ah, grand. Slept well, did she?' Again, showing keen interest in the welfare of baby Enid. 'No nightmares?'

'No, no. She slept right on through. She's been sleeping well recently.'

'Ah, that's good news. Always a hard time for the little ones, you know.' Ms Kiely shuffled a little anxiously and fidgeted with her hands. 'They can sense things. Sorrow and the sort.'

'Oh,' Max said in return, not quite knowing what to make of this superstition. But again, it all seemed to be in support of his child's welfare more than anything else. Perhaps he should have mentioned he was bringing Enid after all. Was there some cultural thing about death and babies that he was unaware of? Maybe the bad phone signal and GPS were a sign that they were further away from home than just a few hundred miles.

'Jesus,' she said. 'I can go on, I know. But do think about what I've said. You've had a look around and seen there's a good amount of things that need sorting. Not much of a holiday for you and the family is it?'

'Well, we had planned on going to the coast for a few days.'

'And what a lovely plan that sounds,' she said, flicking his shoulder. 'I'll tell you what, Maxy, let's get the urgent paperwork signed and then I can even help take care of Carla's myself?' she offered. Max put this down to local hospitality, but he'd feel guilty lumping this all on Ms Kiely.

*I really must ask for her name.*

Not only that, he hadn't been the best brother in the last decade and every moment he spent in Ireland, he felt like he needed to pay back a greater debt than was owed, to make up for his reluctance in letting his sister back into his life. She hadn't even had the chance to meet Enid, and he knew their mother would be turning in her grave at that. He had to make amends himself, even if it was a selfish act now to nothing but the memory of his sister.

'Ms Kiely,' he asked, and she looked eagerly into his eyes, clearly wishing him to take her up on the offer. He was sorry to let her down. 'May I ask for your first name?' This seemed to irritate her, just like she was indeed a school teacher. You never let your pupils know your first name – that would sabotage your position of power. Although it was the avoidance of the proposal that was most likely the real reason for her irritation, she responded politely enough.

'Aoife. Aoife Aisling Kiely.'

Max crunched his brow a bit not quite understanding what she had said.

'A.O.I.F.E. Aoife.' She repeated. 'But you English always get confused when you see it written down. So phonetically it's like, ee-fa.'

'Ee-fa,' Max repeated, feeling himself go red and

hoping he hadn't offended her. He should have just stuck with Ms Kiely.

'Ah, that's good enough, you dummy. Now, will you go ahead and leave it all to me, so?' she asked once again.

'Unfortunately, I think I owe it to my sister to take care of this. But yes, it will take a while, so perhaps we take a holiday and then I return alone. I can take some more time off work. There's no immediate rush is there?'

Without hesitating, Aoife took him up on the offer. 'Then that's that settled. You lads get on over to the coast.' Aoife seemed to relax into that woman in the road once again. 'Absolutely no rush back. Your sister paid all her bills annually, so really you've got until the end of the year. But it does no good to leave a house empty for long, mind you.' She glanced around the hallway as if looking for something to fight off. 'I'll make some calls for you. I know a ton of places down there that *do* accommodate tourists.' She gave Max another flick of the shoulder and then handed him a stack of paperwork she had stashed in her gardening apron.

'Sign and come on down if you have any questions.' Max was a little stunned that she had the paperwork already on her and she didn't shy away from it. 'I've no need for an office in the city when a pen will fit in my pocket. I'll catch up with you later.'

# 8

'She is in a rush to see the back of us isn't she?' Nat said as Max got back in the car, still a bit ruffled that they were leaving as abruptly as they'd come.

Max clicked his seatbelt in, having already stopped off at Aoife's to drop off the paperwork.

'Why is she getting in her car?' Nat asked.

'She said she wanted to see us out,' Max said, a little confused himself.

'Out of the country?'

'Ha. No, just out of the village. Said she had to go somewhere anyway.'

'But–'

'I know, I know,' Max said, raising his hands in surrender. 'But that woman knows what she wants and I'm pretty sure she gets it ninety nine percent of the time.'

Nat still looked confused.

'I think she just likes to keep busy,' Max said.

'Bless her,' Nat said.

Max drove off down the hill, Aoife's large battered

Jeep following promptly behind. Looking in the rear view it was clear that Aoife's car was too big for her small frame. Max could just make out her head poking over the wheel. He chuckled to himself as they went on down towards the forest edge and was reminded of something he had discovered over the paperwork.

'Oh,' he said. 'I found out what Coillte Ádh means.'

Nat only looked half interested but he proceeded on.

'Wood's Lucky,' he said smiling.

'Huh? Wood's Lucky?'

'Yeah, but I'm thinking it's like other languages where it's back to front, you know? Like cat black or car red.'

'So it's Lucky Woods?' Nat said.

'Yeah, or maybe even Lucky's Woods. Kind of like Cable's Wood near us. Not so scary now is it? But really, this must be a forest, it's so dense.' As they approached the exit of the little village, Max went to give it one last look in the mirror but it was blocked off by Aiofe's huge Jeep. 'She's a bit close isn't she?' Max said.

'Oh yeah,' Nat said, looking over her shoulder to check it wasn't a trick of the mirror. 'Very close.'

As they entered the shelter of the trees, Aoife popped her headlights on and, although they weren't full beams, they were rather dazzling due to the raised height of the Jeep against the little Kia.

Max flicked the dimmer over on the mirror and put his own headlights on.

*When in Rome.*

Enid started to stir in the back and within seconds started to sob. By the time they'd reached the bend she was in full blown cry mode. Once again Max heard a pitch that sounded like pain. He eased up off the accelerator and turned to check she was ok, but two sharp blasts of a horn brought his attention right back to the road. He looked back up just in time to see a large deer standing still in the middle of the narrow road, its antlers flanking its head like a human would put their arms out to stop a car. But Max couldn't stop, he was too close. He swerved to avoid it. Struggling on the slack surface, the little Kia lost its grip and Nat let out a sharp scream of fear. Years of driving for a living set Max's autopilot off and he quickly put his foot back onto the accelerator to give the front wheels some grip, helping the car to steady, and onwards they went. He didn't take his foot off the accelerator again until they were out the other side of the woods.

Aoife, the owner of the phantom beeps it turned out, got out of her Jeep as they pulled over at the junction that would take them on to their new destination.

Max got out to say goodbye but asked Nat to stay in the car with Enid and she happily obliged.

'Fecking deer,' Aoife said. Max was taken aback once again by the way her tone could transform from that of a polished solicitor to this sprightly manner at the drop of a hat. 'That's why I drive that big tank.' She thumbed back to the Jeep. 'Deer always standing around in the road like bowling pins waiting to be struck. Eejits. Anyway, you go and enjoy your holiday and I'll be seeing you again when you fancy it. Next week's grand or if you'd rather go home first and freshen up it doesn't bother me a bit.' At that, she opened her arms for a hug and Max couldn't help but feel gratitude towards this new force of nature that had entered his life. Once again he was able to understand why his sister had loved it there.

He leaned in and gave her a quick squeeze, looking

absently back at the battered Jeep as he did. He noticed right away that only one headlamp was switched on. Before he could question it, Aoife gave him a flick on the shoulder and sent him on his way. He wanted to double check again in the rear view but thought better of it, not wanting Nat to hear of the deer's likely sad demise at the hands of the Jeep. Besides, the Jeep had seen better days. Maybe it was faulty. He flicked an indicator on, pulled out and headed on down to the Atlantic under a belt of cloud that looked as if it was fit to burst with rain.

# 9

Max felt a tug in his gut as he watched Nat and Enid's plane take off from the small Galway car park. He had decided to stay on alone after their short coastal holiday and had had no problems getting signal to phone ahead to Aoife. Everything was arranged. This was the first time he had been away from Enid and he hadn't really thought about how he'd feel emotionally. It was shit already. Max turned to his new hire car to try and cheer himself up. After a complaint about the fuel and broken boot, they had upgraded him to the saloon class for free, but he had asked for an estate instead. He might need the extra room in the coming days.

He got behind the wheel of the new roomy Skoda and started playing with all the knobs and dials. By the time he was on the main road he felt guiltily like an eligible bachelor, rather than a man who had just left his wife and child and was on the way to clean up his dead sister's house. Not caring for the health of the car, Max popped it into sport mode and pushed the bigger engine around the country roads. He was having so much fun that he forgot to look out for the village from the road, to see how they'd missed it the other day. Regardless, his years of taxi driving didn't get him lost.

Without Enid's bizarre crying, Max was able to take in some of the foliage as he drove back through the forest. When they were younger, there was a game their father had always played with them. They had to guess as many trees as they could, and the winner would get to work the gears on the car while their father drove. It had certainly given Max a solid knowledge of trees to call upon. The forest was predominately made up of oaks and beeches, but there was plenty hidden here, and soon he'd brought the car down to a crawl to look deeper at the mix. He could make out healthy ashes, rowans with their berries, Scots pine dotted here and there among groups of hawthorn and he was sure there were some hazels.

Seeing the end of the forest road in sight, Max decided to pull over to the side and get out for a few minutes. The air was surprisingly salty considering how inland they were, but it brought with it a crispness which felt odd in such a dense forest. Perhaps he still had some salt up his nose from the coast. Max took a deep breath and closed his eyes, listening to the sounds of the forest. Had Carla ever come walking around here? When they were younger, Carla had been his guide whenever their parents had been too busy – one benefit of an older sibling. Having more time to digest their father's knowledge, Carla was able to show Max how the prevailing winds shaped the trees, which were the south-westerlies in Sussex; how to tell if an incline was hard to climb, owning to a narrow path; and, although he'd never needed it, how to locate the

North Star – Polaris. He didn't get too much reminiscing in, as he was abruptly startled out of his thoughts by a gruff voice.

'What are you doing in here?' it said.

Max looked round to find the source and focused on some dense treeline.

'Max, isn't it?' This time the voice came from a completely different direction and Max turned to see his late sister's neighbour walking towards him. He had an expression of disapproval on his face, which Max thought was a bit too much considering he was a grown man, not some punk kid.

*I must check his name too.*

'I'm just having a look. David isn't it?' Max replied.

'A look for what?' he said, coming closer and ignoring the question.

'I, I dunno. I just like trees I guess.' Max wondered if that sounded as stupid to David as it did to him.

'You just like trees, so?' David repeated back. Turns out it must have sounded stupid. 'Well, it does no good looking in these woods if you don't know what you're looking for. You'll easily get lost.' This was only the second time he'd seen David yet they'd certainly graduated from polite condolent nods. At a loss for words, Max thought he'd try the trees again.

'It's a *wood* then is it?'

'Were you expecting a city?'

'No, I just thought it looked a bit… foresty,' Max said.

David seemed to ponder this. 'Ah, Jesus. Well, I've no idea about what makes a wood and what makes a forest but, I'm not the reading type. This here is Coillte Ádh. Lucky's Woods.'

'So it is that way round,' Max said to himself.

'What's that now?'

'Nothing,' Max said, wishing David would move on, but instead he came closer, inspecting Max like an object in a museum.

'Well, it's a good job you're here as I need to get back up the hill to open up and you've got that shiny new car to take me there, haven't you?' This clearly wasn't a question as David walked by Max towards the Skoda as if the matter was settled. The trees were calling Max, but not wanting to annoy his immediate neighbour, which might prove unwise when he came to sell Carla's house, he followed suit.

They got into the car together and David started inspecting it from the inside as Max drove off. David didn't bother with his seatbelt until the car reminded him to put it on. 'Bloody things. Talk too much these days,' he said.

'What were you looking for?' Max asked in a much more polite manner than David had.

David cranked his neck to Max but did most of his staring with his eyeballs, which felt a little aggressive, but as they broke through the woods, he smiled and looked back up the road.

'Ah, well. I suppose I stuck my nose in your business so you've a right to ask me what mine was,' David said. Digging into his jacket pockets he pulled out a handful of hazelnuts.

'Oh, so they were hazels?'

'Jesus, you weren't lying about liking trees,' David said and dropped the handful into the cup holder on the centre console. 'Go up past ours,' he said, pointing past

34

their houses as Max approached. They wound up the hill and were soon in the little square he, Nat and Enid had zipped through on arrival. He pointed out to the small closed pub and Max pulled up outside.

'You'll pop in one night will ya, Maxy?'

'Sure,' Max said.

'Grand.' David gave him one last up and down, then nodded in approval. Turns out he lived next to the local landlord. How soon would it be before they all called him "tree boy"?

## 10

Max let the needle drop onto the vinyl and heard the satisfying crackle and pop issue from the speakers before it found the first groove. John Lennon's voice filled the room. "I Dig a Pygmy, by Charles Hawtrey and the Deaf Aids. Phase One, in which Doris gets her oats!" Max smiled at the familiar sentence, yet he still had no idea what it was about, and vowed never to find out. Some things were better left a mystery, he thought.

He hadn't got far on the clear up operation since dropping off David earlier, but he had at least put a plan in place. There were to be three piles: keep for himself; donate to the locals and charity, if they wanted it; straight to tip, wherever that was round here. So far, Carla's box of vinyl had safely parked itself in the *Keep* pile and that's about all he'd done. He was flicking through the record sleeves, some of which he had actually attended the purchase of.

That short-lived bachelor feeling had definitely been left somewhere on the side of the N59 and now he was in full mourning and regret mode. Max realised he had been carrying around a good wedge of shame for the way he had treated his sister, and letting himself mourn in front of Nat, as close as they were, felt far too hypocritical. Alone in Carla's house, with her records playing, it all started to come out and he imagined this is how he should have felt back in England when he'd received the call from Aoife. She was right, this was how it should be done.

He was halfway through *I've got a Feeling* when he came across the vinyl for Nirvana's *Nevermind*. Ordinarily, he would have been chuffed about finding this somewhere like a bargain bucket, but this particular copy, if it was the one he suspected, was extra special. He pulled the inner sleeve out with a quivering hand and was greeted with the smiling young faces of the band. His eyes scanned the top and his heart gave a little skip. It was the copy he thought it was.

He had gone with his sister to the local record store in Furlong when he was just thirteen, as she was raving about this new band. Carla always had her finger on the pulse with music and promised him it would be worth the trip. After a short shared listen at the store, she bought two copies of the record and handed one to Max: his first ever record. He guiltily remembered his reaction at the time to being handed a vinyl record and not a CD – it was 1991 after all. Unfortunately, Max's, or really their mother's, record player was playing records at a slower and slower pace at that point in time, so it was Carla's copy that had done the hard graft. Replay after replay, whenever Max had been over, which was quite often back then. After several listens of it together, Max was hooked. He wasn't sure of all the exact lyrics but it didn't stop him singing

37

along. One day, Carla added Max's name to the band line-up on the sleeve as "backing vocals." In her dead straight handwriting it was hard to tell the difference from the official print, and there it still was, albeit a little faded along with the rest of it. She'd always had a knack with calligraphy and drawing. He held it up to the light, admiring the indentation of her penwork, and ran a finger lightly over the top to feel its ridges with his fleshy finger, just like a needle would on vinyl.

He pulled the record out, happy to cut off Sir Paul mid chorus when a few sheets of paper spilled out that he wasn't familiar with. He shook out the sleeve to see if anything else was inside, then carefully replaced the vinyl and picked up the sheets to inspect. The Beatles played on. He immediately knew they were his sister's drawings but he had to keep rotating them in his hands until he got the perspective.

They were of a forest, a forest filled with oaks, rowans with their berries, hawthorns and the occasional pine. Carla had captured their trunks and leaf structures perfectly and, even in this pencil sketch, he thought them worthy of a place in any tree identification book. Some pages showed the forest in its entirety while others were macro vignettes of leaves and bark. His earlier question of whether his sister had walked in the woods had been answered, although it was clear she had done more than walking.

Max didn't find her fascination odd at all. After all, their father had been a ranger, and there had always been textbooks lying about and many a day spent in the back of their dad's Defender when they struggled to get childcare. *Ah, the eighties.* Max pulled up perhaps the fullest and most intricate of the sheets which showed one of the full landscape sketches. His fingers went off again, feeling over the sheet, taking in the depth of the sketched areas until they came to rest on the edge of an oak trunk. There, poking out from the side, camouflaged in the same graphite grey, was a deer's head looking straight at him with one of its eyes. Its grey colour had been shaded over many times and the shimmer of the residual graphite made it catch the light as a real deer's would. He wasn't sure how long he'd been having a stare down with this sketched mammal, but soon enough his senses were brought back into the room by the crackling of a record that needed changing.

## 11

It had just gone eight in the evening when Max stepped into the pub. It seemed that this might be where all the unfriendly locals hung out, as there were no waves and smiles like the other day. As they probably all knew David well, it didn't surprise Max too much. Still, it was unsettling walking up to the bar alone feeling like he was hushing them in his wake. The ceiling was quintessentially low and the bar formed a small U-shape, inviting many to the available stools, but it was the tables that were full – each with a clear view of him. He took up a seat at the edge of the bar and decided to give it five minutes before faking a call and running right back out the door. He unzipped his windbreaker and realised he'd never been so hot in summer, or thirsty.

'Alright, alright, you lot,' said a gruff familiar voice from behind.

Max turned around to see David scooching along a bench and leaving a couple of men – and a drink – behind at a table.

'Yes, it's Carla's brother. Now go back to your pints and slagging off Joe's last batch of lambs.'

There was a ripple of deep chuckles across the room.

David got behind the bar and gave his signature nod to Max as he pulled down a pint glass from above. He gave a good couple of tugs on the tap handle and placed the dark pint on the bar. Max would be having a stout apparently.

He went to pull out his wallet but David raised a hand.

'For the ride back,' he said. 'How's that sorting going?'

Max thanked him and took a sip of the stout. He was surprised at its sweet note, and clearly this showed on his face as David gave another nod and grunt in response.

'I made some piles.'

'And what are you putting in those piles? Wood?'

'Because of the trees? Very good. No, I haven't got that far yet. I was going to ask if there was anything you or anyone else wanted?'

David looked away as if it hurt him somewhat.

Max tried to recover. 'Furniture really. You know, big things. Must be easier than dragging it out the village, the big stuff.'

'Some of us saps do have cars, you know.'

Feeling like he might always be on the backfoot with David unless he showed some backbone, Max pushed his welcome and fought back. 'You should get one David, then I wouldn't need to taxi you around.'

David's expression didn't change for a moment, which wasn't all that uncommon Max had gathered in the short time he'd known David, but then he cracked a toothy smile. 'There you are, ha. Good craic.' David looked across to his table where his half empty pint lay, clicked

41

his tongue and poured himself a fresh one from the tap. He nudged Max's glass with it and quietly said, 'To Carla.'

'To Carla,' Max replied, feeling his eyes prickle.

*Not here.*

As they took their sips, the door opened and Max, now feeling like he belonged a little more, was able to enjoy someone else entering the pub this time.

A frail man walked in with a limp and a bandage around his right hand. The lighting was low in the pub but Max thought he could make out blood stains behind the otherwise white wrapping. It looked like a fresh accident.

'Davidy, Davidy,' he said, approaching the bar with a grin on his face. 'Pour us out a couple will you?'

'Glenn. I've told you to stop coming round here spending a grand until you're blind,' David said, leaving Max to his drink and heading to the middle of the bar.

'Ah, pish. I know you need the money.'

'No, it's you that needs the money, you gobshite. We all know that,' David said.

That ripple of grunting David-like laughter came again from the surrounding tables.

'If you go to one of those shops out of town you'll get yourself a whole bottle of gin for the price of a few of my beers.'

Glenn flapped away the comment with his good hand. 'Ah, no. I don't *need* to go out of town, David. Not when you run a perfectly good establishment here. Besides, who's gonna take me there? Are *you* gonna drive me, so?' said the man, chuckling at his own wit. It looked as if David didn't drive after all, but Max knew better than to chip in and mock his only friend in the pub.

'I'll give you one,' David said, raising a finger just to make sure the man had understood.

'Now me and the good people here all know you say one, but you'll soon forget it and then I'll have another one. So pour me two now,' he said, slapping some change on the bar. Max couldn't make out how much, due to the change in currency, but David quickly enough scooped it off and pocketed it.

David thought it over and Max wondered how often this scene had played out, as no one else in the pub was paying attention to this interaction anymore.

'Well, there's no sense in a stale pint,' David said, pulling down a glass and filling it up from a different tap than the one he'd used for their drinks. He slid the paler pint across the bar to Glenn and left him to his devices, returning to Max.

Taking his seat, Glenn cradled the pint with both his good and bandaged hand, and brought it up to his lips, smacking them together when he was done. 'That's a batch that, David,' Glenn said, not taking his eyes off the pint.

'It's watered down piss you tool,' David mumbled into his own pint, but Glenn was too occupied to hear him.

Max scrunched his brow at David.

'Don't worry, lad,' David said. 'You've got the proper stuff. Glenn's got the devil in him when it comes to drinking, and in truth I'd rather keep him in here drinking my special draught than anywhere else where he could do damage. I just have to make him work for it or he'll go getting suspicious.'

Max took a glug of his own pint which was a lot darker than the one David had given to Glenn.

'Imagine if he did get hold of the hard stuff, *that* would be some damage.'

'Looks like he's already done some damage to himself,' Max said, gesturing to the bandages.

'Yeah, well. That's his business,' David said. Now it was him that was talking to his pint and avoiding Max's eyes.

## 12

Max's eyes didn't sting as he opened the curtains in the spare room. He had woken up around four this time, and for the last hour he'd just been staring at the ceiling thinking about Carla. She really seemed to have had a nice life here. Unfortunately, Max knew it could have been that bit sweeter for her if he'd been a better brother. Paradise was no good with a thorn in your side that you couldn't pluck out.

He went through the quiet house to the kitchen and filled up his glass with fresh water, gulping it away quickly then refilling for a second one. The water sure didn't taste bad here. He had stayed on for a few more drinks at the pub. The locals had slowly made their way over to offer their condolences and tell him how lovely his sister had been. Not one of them asked why he had never visited or why he didn't attend the funeral. It only added to his guilt, and the hangover wasn't helping.

His head swayed thinking about the amount of beer he had consumed. He only hoped David had been sneaky enough to swap him on to Glenn's lighter keg without his knowing. Max moved over to the stack of records looking for something soothing to put on, then he saw Carla's drawings once again. He wondered if she had any more knocking around the place, or *hiding* around the place perhaps. *Why had she put them in the sleeve?* He picked up the one with the deer and studied it while he gulped down his water. The deer stared back silently. Not really in the mood for breakfast yet, and certainly not in the mood to get on with sorting out Carla's belongings, he made his way back into the bedroom, got changed, grabbed the drawing and headed out the back door and through the gate.

He looked down at the tree line from where the path opened up and guessed the forest was just short of a mile away. It was still early and he didn't want to wake up the locals with any engine noise, so made his way down the hill on foot. He was there sooner than he expected, having jogged down the steeper bits of hill then cut through the fenceless fields as the crow flies towards the end. The forest was humming with the sound of birds eager to start their day, he smiled and took what looked like a well-trodden path near to the dirt roadside.

He followed the path until he came to a fork. He could still make out the road to his left so took a right to go deeper into the forest. He made a mental note of the turn but David's words about getting lost rang in his ears, so he promised himself not to take too many forks – orientation was harder with a hangover. In his mid-teens Max spent many nights drinking in the South Downs with his friends. It was easy to get lost in minutes when the sun went down and they'd often wake up in fields that hadn't been there the night before. It made for some argumentative scenes the following morning when bellies were rumbling and heads were heavy.

Within a few minutes he had lost sight of the road and came to a clearing which had a number of paths leading from it, each looking like the last one he'd taken. His heart beat a little faster at the thought of disobeying David. He turned on his heels and studied the path he had just walked along. There was stubby pine at head height just beside him, something none of the other paths had.

'Scots pine, Scots pine, Scots pine,' he chanted to himself. He made his way into the middle of clearing and felt in his back pocket for Carla's drawing. He thought that if he could find the place she had drawn, it might help to fill some of the time they had lost together. Shared memories, different times.

Just as his fingertips gripped the paper he heard a rustling to the side and snapped his head in the direction of the sound so fast he cricked his neck. He wanted to reach up and massage the area but he was frozen still, with his heart somewhere between his throat and nose.

There, standing head on, near one of the pathways, was a deer. Quickly scanning through his father's books in his head, Max supposed it was a red deer due to its size and lack of spots. It didn't have antlers, and considering the time of year, Max thought it might be a hind. Just as he'd lost track of time looking at his sister's drawing of a deer the other night, Max wasn't sure how long they stood looking at each other. Every now and again, it twitched an ear, flared its nostrils or shook its head quickly to fling off some unwanted pests. Otherwise, it stood dead still watching him, puffs of warm breath leaving its snout and dissipating in the cool morning air. Not being an artist like Carla was, Max slowly went into his pocket after a time to get his phone out and take a photo.

*Nat would love this.*

Maybe Enid would too when she grew to understand a bit better. The deer didn't seem to mind this new motion and as he pulled the phone up to unlock its screen it once again failed him and froze at his touch.

'Oh fuck off.' He tried to click the locker on and off but it was no good. It would need a full restart again and rather than waste time on that he thought he'd try and enjoy the moment the old fashioned way a little longer.

## 13

After a while, the deer moved on and Max was struck with a sense of awe at the encounter he'd just had. He'd never laid eyes on a wild deer for longer than a few seconds in all his life, and he'd spent a *lot* of time outdoors. Yet, this one had let him have his fill until *it* was bored enough to carry on with its day. Had Carla perhaps drawn the same deer? A conceited individual that stood still until the artist finished off their work? Same deer or not, he counted himself lucky and pompously thought the deer had perhaps ascertained he was no threat and, "of good heart".

He turned and made his way back past the stubby pine with a smile on his face. If he bumped into David again he could answer that smarmy question with an answer; he had found what he was looking for, an experience shared with Carla. They had shared a moment somehow. He found the fork in the path near the road once again and made out towards the forest edge which was now back in view. He was just making it through a narrow thicket of shrubs and overhanging branches when he heard more rustling to his side. He was careful not to snap his head so quickly this time, and he thought it a bloody good job he hadn't, as he was faced with another deer – but this one a mere arms reach away. The deer looked at him side on.

*What is going on in this forest?*

Max took in the creature and concluded this was no Bambi. It was a full grown stag like the one he'd dodged in the road. He now realised that what he'd thought were overhanging branches while wistfully strolling along in awe of his previous encounter, were actually the deer's antlers. They just pipped him for height. Max struggled to keep his composure, disbelieving in his luck to see two deer, and two super chill ones at that. He was close enough to this one to smell its musty pelt! It was standing just off the path, but had it not made a noise, Max would have strolled right by it. He tried to swallow and push his heart back down into his chest but it didn't want to hear of it. He didn't try his phone again and simply stared back into the deer's eye with both of his own, hypnotised. Then a stupid thought crept into his head: *pet it.*

*No, don't pet it. It's wild!*

He wasn't entirely sure when humans had gained the impulse to pet anything that was remotely fluffy, but he felt it burning now. Slowly he raised his left hand upwards but kept it close to his chest. He wiggled his fingers to ensure the deer had seen it. As it was seemingly unphased, Max slowly reached out and placed his palm on the nose like he would if it was a horse. The deer gave a single blink as if allowing the action. Max gave it a rub up and down, short at first, but eventually making it all the way from the tip of the nose up between its ears. It was up here he felt something a bit strange under his fingertips. It was cold and wet. He slowly removed his hand and brought it up to his face to see what he'd stuck his fingers in. He saw a thick dark substance on his little and ring fingers. He massaged some of it together with his thumb and found it rather tacky and also a bit gristly. His eyes already knew it was blood but they were taking a while to fire the signal back to his brain.

The deer turned to face him head on and when Max looked up he thought he might throw up, or faint, or shit himself, or all of the above, for the other side of the deer's head was caved in and sodden with blood.

Where there should have been another eye there was only a bloody crater, its surface crawling with maggots. The side of its jaw was ripped open, revealing a row of shattered teeth and exposed jawbone. The opposite antlers looked as if they'd been struck by lightning; the symmetry was gone, replaced only by shards of blackening bone and ripped velvet. Aoife *did* hit something in her Jeep: *this* deer. The quick remorse he felt for the deer left him in an instant as his brain now caught up and became baffled at how this thing could still be alive, and standing at that. It *wasn't* possible.

To prove it was indeed alive, the deer suddenly lurched its head forward like a viper and snapped at Max's hand taking his two bloody fingers with a crack of bone that he heard deep inside his own skull.

He went to scream but only managed a dull noise and fell backwards off the path into the scrub.

The deer jostled its head around twirling his fingertips in its mouth like balls in a raffle. Somewhere through the ringing in his ears Max heard the crunch of the deer's jagged teeth obliterating his fingers to powder.

Max looked down at the severed stalks that remained on his shaking hand.

*This isn't happening.*

He gave one a wiggle. The pain surged and the blood began spurting.

*This is happening.*

As the deer finished its mouthful, a powerful hoof thumped down on the path and Max's adrenaline kicked in.

He rose to his feet in a flash, grasping the little stumps with his free hand, and broke through the short stretch of forest and onto the road. The feel of compact dirt underfoot gave him some gusto and he burst into a full sprint heading for the treeline which was only a stone's throw away. He didn't dare look back but his ears picked up the heavy gallop of hooves that faded just as he broke through the treeline and into the sun. Max was no runner, but seemingly his legs had been waiting for this day and he kicked dust back up to the village. His pulse thumped in his ears and his left hand now felt very cold from keeping it compressed and aloft. He got back to the path behind Carla's house just in time to bump into David who took one look at him with a face like thunder.

## 14

'What the feck were you doing down in those woods you eejit?' David said while frantically looking through his cupboards. Max did have an answer for this but couldn't remember what it was right now. 'I told you not to go into them. Didn't I tell you?'

Max had sunk deeply into David's sofa and was now clutching a bandage David had quickly whipped on. He listened to David's words but struggled to focus.

*I'm going to faint.*

Had he even told David that's where he had been?

*Chocolate. I need chocolate.*

'It does no good for anyone being in those woods,' David continued.

The room was swimming now. Had he lost a lot of blood? How much could you lose from a couple of fingers? Was he going to die?

*Oh fuck, I'm going to die.*

*You're not going to die.*

Max tried to take some deep breaths, his lips flapping loosely with the effort of the exhale.

David came into focus unwrapping something in his hands. He gave it a snap and then thrust it under Max's nose.

His eyes stung and the shock caused him to inhale sharply, which brought with it a fresh sharp aroma of ammonia that ran deep into his lungs and brought his senses alive.

'I said, I fucking said. Those woods are good for nothing. Fucking, Lucky.'

Max didn't think he was so lucky.

*My fingers. My bloody fingers.*

'You didn't say not to go in,' Max managed to squeeze out of his lungs, now assuming he must have told David about the forest in his shock and forgotten.

'What?' David said, tossing the broken stick into his lap.

'You said—'

'You're a smart enough man to figure my meaning. Those woods are bad.'

'But you...' he tried again like a child scorned. 'It's a fucking forest.'

'They're bad, Maxy.' Max tried to make sense of what David was saying but the mix of blood loss and smelling salts had sent him giddy. 'And sneaking out!'

'I wasn't sneaking,'

'Not sneaking? Then why didn't you take your car down, so? Why did you go early? Why were you skulking around the back?'

Max wanted to explain that he'd done it out of courtesy, but now he was stunned that he had to explain himself at all. He was a grown man and he could go where he pleased.

'I should have kept a closer eye on you after the first time,' David said. 'Ah, Jesus. You're white as a sheet, you must have been pissing blood all up the hill. You're gonna have to go down to the day hospital and I can't bloody well drive you.' David paced back and forth in the room. 'Gonna have to get her.'

'Who?' Max said, his head lightly buzzing. It felt like he was watching a drama on TV and he was interested in how this scene would end.

David shot him one last scolding glare and then left the room. Max heard several doors slam in his wake.

Max sat there breathing heavily and looked down at the bandage.

*I've just lost two of my fingers.*

The sight brought renewed pain into his receptors and, along with the salts, it helped him get a better grip on things. Blood was visible but it looked more white dotted with red than the other way around. He shifted in his seat and felt a crinkling under one of his bum cheeks. He reached down with his free hand and pulled out a folded slip of paper from his back pocket. Was this all real? He unfolded the sheet as best he could with one hand and looked down at his sister's drawing. His eyes searched over the well shaded trunk and foliage until they came to rest on the head of the deer as it poked out from the tree. It looked as harmless as any drawing could be, as any deer could be, yet he found himself wary of that one shining graphite eye. What was on the other side of *this* deer's head? What thoughts were running through its paper brain? Would it take a chunk out of his other hand, a papercut even? With the horror building he flicked the sheet aside and let it fall to the floor.

This was just a wild coincidence. Wild indeed was the word. He had tried to pet a wild animal, should he have expected anything else? Humans had been killing deer for centuries; maybe this one wanted some retribution. But there was of course a bigger mystery here, one that he'd been trying to ignore: how was that deer still standing? His hazy mind didn't struggle to bring forward some choice snaps of its caved-in skull, a skull that may well have been damaged only a few days prior by Aoife's Jeep.

*It couldn't be the same deer; it would have bled out by now.*

Max's head started to pound once again at these thoughts and soon the colour dropped out of his vision.

A few more pounding sounds and David returned bringing Aoife.

She started talking but Max thought it best to shut his eyes.

A moment later he was on his feet and moving.

He was on some cold leather seats.

Then, well, then he couldn't make out much of anything.

## 15

Max came out of the day hospital with a feeling of embarrassment he hadn't felt in a long time. After the initial examination, the doctor had wagered he'd only lost about half a pint of blood after the prompt clotting by his platelets. Any fainting was purely down to personal preference. After goading Max, saying that people lost more blood when they volunteered to donate, the doctor surveyed what remained of Max's severed fingers one last time. He commented on the lucky, almost surgical, precision in which the fingers had parted company with the rest of his hand, snapped off his gloves and left the nurse to clean up.

Aoife was in the waiting room, seemingly deep in a magazine featuring a collection of farmers on the front, sheep dogs restlessly at heel. Even in the photo it was clear they wanted to be off herding sheep. David was nowhere to be seen. She looked up at Max approaching and, unlike David's face earlier, hers only showed concern and friendliness.

'Ah, there you are, love.' She glanced down to his hands instantly. 'All cleaned up I see.'

'Yes,' Max said, raising his hand slightly. It gave a little throb in return but the painkillers he'd been given quickly washed it away. He felt a deep gratitude for Aoife, tinged with shame for his fainting. 'Thank you so much for driving me down here. I hope I didn't bleed in your Jeep too much.' He looked out through the windows for its large burgundy frame.

'Ah stop, it's no bother. That thing has been through a lot. If I do find any drops it'll wipe right off,' she said. Max wondered how easily the deer had wiped off. Ask about the deer, that annoying little voice said. It was getting bolshier by the day.

*No. If she even did hit the deer, she could have just had a light out.*

'I'm just ever so sorry for your fingers, Maxy. We should have warned you that the wildlife around here is a little... nibbly.' She gave her shoulders a little shrug as if to make nothing of it. 'They're not to be fed and petted like horses.'

'Yes, well. It *is* a wild animal after all. My fault,' he said, ignoring the fact he wasn't actually trying to feed it, although it had received a snack nonetheless.

*But you did try and pet it.*

'And the doctor didn't—'

'I said it was a power tool accident,' Max said. After coming to his senses a bit more, and realising that the doctor wasn't concerned about the decapitation from a medical point of view, Max decided to lie. It just seemed easier to lie. He didn't want to bring their little village under attack from any public health services.

'That's grand,' she said, almost beaming. 'In fact,' she continued, putting the magazine aside and leading Max out, 'you might be surprised, or not surprised now, to see that there's a few fingers missing around town, bunch of dopes that we are.'

'Yes, I did see—'

'That eejit Glenn?'

'Yes, it was.' Max found it odd that Aoife was able to pinpoint the man so easily. Or was she just seeing him off? Was it really common practice to go around losing digits, and be known for it at that? Surely the locals, if anyone, would know not to try and stroke a deer twice. Bite me once, shame on me, bite me twice – that might be all my fingers gone, Max thought, looking down at his own.

The fresh air was helpful in bringing Max up a couple of notches as they stepped outside. There was a strong breeze and it whipped around them as they headed to the Jeep. Aoife wasn't lying about the state of the Jeep. Now, truly paying attention it was clear this Jeep had received some dings. Who was to say if that broken headlight was a new addition?

He tried to unlink the Jeep and the deer and brought his thoughts back to Carla's place. He realised he was now faced with the task of clearing Carla's house with a dud hand, and what on earth was Nat going to say? What was *he* going to say? At least the deer hadn't taken the ring off his finger too – that was now safely on his other hand. On the drive back, his mind nagged on. As much as he tried to ignore it, it wouldn't drop the image of the deer with half a head. It wasn't the horrific nature of the image, it was the reality of it. It could simply be that he'd been seeing things, riding a euphoric Dr. Dolittle train that had some hallucinogenic side effects with his hangover.

He considered for a moment the notion that he had indeed imagined the caved in head of the deer then took Aoife's explanation, as weird as it sounded, as gospel. There was also Glenn, a *local,* who may have lost his fingers in the same manner. David said he was a drunk – perhaps he'd forgotten and tried to feed a deer some hazelnuts, not that deer couldn't feed themselves. Even a cow will eat grass out of your hand if you offer it. Finally, there was the fact that the deer seemed to be very, very tame. Max had two close encounters in the space of five minutes, after forty years of seeing deer run in the other direction from across a field.

Aoife didn't speak of it anymore on the drive back, instead filling him in on her plans for Christmas, oddly enough. Max continued to chew over the facts quietly while half listening. He didn't even get to look at Coillte Ádh from the road as he'd meant to do. By the time they got back, he had been prepared to let the whole thing go. He put it down to grief, stress and missing his wife and child. That was until he stepped back into Carla's house and found David sitting in the kitchen with Carla's drawing in his hands.

## 16

'Errr, hi David,' Max said, stopping near the entrance to the kitchen.

David looked up and nodded, then returned to look down at the drawing as if he belonged in the house.

'Shall I put the kettle on?' Max offered, not sure how to deal with the situation.

'Ah no, you're alright lad, I've just made one,' he said, gesturing once again with that swiss army nod of his.

Max didn't move to make one for himself.

'I loved her, you know,' David said, continuing to study the drawing. 'She was so talented, your sister. Always creating. She even turned gardening into an art. I used to look out my upstairs window every morning to see what she'd been up to the day before. It always put a smile on my face. The way she'd train things to grow, the places she decided to plant, even the way she raked the leaves. It was magical.'

'Our father was a ranger,' Max said, sharing a fact he had no need to tell this man.

David chuckled at this. 'I know.'

Max felt uncomfortable. He wasn't sure why but he shifted down to the drawers at the end of the worktop where he recalled some particularly sharp kitchen utensils.

'What did you ask for, Maxy?' David said, finally looking up. Max hadn't asked anyone for anything, what was David on about?

'Sorry?' he replied, his heart beating at this strange question while his good hand fumbled behind him for the handle of the drawer.

'I thought about letting this go, you know. Everyone around here said it wasn't connected. That it had nothing to do with the woods, nothing to do with *her*. Of course they would ignore it, the gombeens. But after seeing this,' David said, shaking the sheet of paper with one hand, 'I don't think I'm right to let it go. I think that would be doing Carla a disservice. Carla asked for something and I think it cost her her life.'

Max's hand stopped searching for the handle and suddenly he didn't feel threatened anymore in his vulnerable state. What had David said? Carla asked who for *what* and paid with her *life*?

'David,' Max started, but stopped when he locked eyes with David. He was crying, and not the type of crying where the tears sat in the eye. They were pouring down his face, following the contours and wrinkles that came with age.

'I knew something was up.' David managed to squeeze out. 'She'd changed alright since her wife died, anyone would, but that's years ago now. She had us around, she had me if she needed me. But those last couple of days… all those walks she did alone, she never wanted me to come. She stopped coming down the pub, stopped gardening, stopped too much and too fast.'

'David, I'm not following. She was sick, wasn't she?'

'Oh, she was sick alright. Because that fucking thing made her sick. It got under her skin, just like it's under Glenn's now. Like it eventually does to everyone who's wanting,'

'Who are you talking about?' Max asked, thinking someone had brought his sister's life to an end before it had been destined to.

'There's a reason Aoife wanted your little one gone, Maxy. She was wise to follow you out. Did she cry when you went through? I bet she did.' Tears were still coming down his face in a steady stream as he went on. Chills had started to crawl up Max's legs, and his balls had long gone into hibernation by the time it reached the bottom of his spine. How did David know about Enid's crying?

'There's a reason you don't see any kids running around up here. There's a reason why some people have got a finger or two missing. Why there's a few more people blind or deaf than there should be in a community this size? Probably why there's a wheelchair in the hall just there. It's more than luck of the draw.' The tears continued.

'David, what happened to my sister?'

'She was fucking killed. Murdered!'

'What? By who?' Max asked, ready to grab whatever he could in the drawers and hunt down the culprit.

'By the woods. By her. That fucking Aos Sí or whatever it fucking is. A leprechaun for all I know. By Lucky.' David finally finished, collapsing with grief back into the seat. Max wasn't entirely sure he'd heard him right. Was he using the word leprechaun in a derogatory sense? Well, of course he must be. What kind of name was Lucky? Was that the owner of the woods, or the village?

But then his subconscious brought forward a host of evidence it had been quietly gathering: the village of Coillte Ádh, at least four-hundred metres in elevation yet invisible from the road; Aoife's bloodied Jeep and her aloof attitude towards losing digits; the deer's head, crushed and bloody; but mostly, Enid's haunted screams. It still rang in his ears with that dreadful pitch of pain. It all became very real. So real that Max let out his own scream in harmony.

## 17

David suggested Max have a cup of tea and they now sat together on Carla's sofa looking out onto her garden. Each sip reduced Max's goosebumps, and soon after, he got his breathing back on track. Max had stopped David from getting more smelling salts – he could still feel the burn in his sinuses from the previous time. Max admired Carla's handiwork in the garden while the omniscient sunshine created harsh shadows, cutting the garden into segments of day and night.

'She's always been here,' David said, 'protecting her woods. Giving the locals what they want. But mostly causing mischief I say. I know how it sounds Maxy, to an outsider, but I'm *not* one of the crazy ones. I've always kept my distance. Until late that is.'

Max sat quietly, minding his tea and staring down at the drawings Carla had done. He'd got them out for David to see.

'Do you know much Irish folklore?' David asked.

Max shook his head, choosing to remain silent.

'I'll start at the beginning then. We were told stories growing up about the people of the mounds: the Aos Sí. Told the stories safely away from this place in nearby Rinavore. It's a second home to us where those expecting little ones retreat to. Most don't lay eyes on the woods until they're past twenty, a little earlier if you come back with your parents. Some never see it – the university lot who go straight to the cities – but I was never much of a good student. Anyway, it's mostly tales of sorts you've heard before, full of fairies and elves, foreign invaders driving the natives underground, giving them sacrifices. But all that stopped a good while back, and now they appease us, or at least that's the way around these eejits think it is. But they never give without taking, especially with Lucky,' David finished and motioned towards Max's bandaged hand. 'So, what did you ask for?'

'Huh?' Max stared down at his bandaged hand and thought the loss was unimportant next to the news of Carla's murder. He still had many questions before they got to the subject of his dearly departed fingers. 'David, who's Lucky?'

'She's what's wrong with those woods. It's her home.' Seeing he'd have to go on some more, David continued. 'She's like a spirit of the woods, its guardian. She's an ecosystem of sacrifice and wishes, and sadly she doesn't go hungry for long, because humans are weak and always wanting.'

'You're talking about fairy tales, David. Supernatural nonsense.'

'Ah, stop. Do your fingers feel like they're in a fairy tale, Maxy? Do you think they're hiding somewhere, or I've got them in my pocket here for you? When have you ever been near an animal that's not tame? I bet you've not touched anything more than a dog or a cat that was happy to? Sure, they can go for you. But did they ever take off two fingers like a butcher? I would think that's evidence enough.'

Max kept fighting the urge to reject all this nonsense, but knowing that Carla was wrapped up in this, he kept his mind open. Maybe there was a wish-granting fairy in the woods?

'So, it's a spirit, this Lucky? There's no body, no manifestation.'

'Why, you want to run her through with a silver spear yourself, do you?'

'Would that work?' Max asked, suddenly distracted.

David smiled back and simply said he didn't know.

'You said leprechaun earlier. That I do know.'

'And what is it that you know lad?' David asked.

Max was about to confidently burst into explanations of jolly little men with pots of gold and likely stray into territories of cultural insult, so decided to button up once again.

David nodded as if he had expected this. 'Some think it's a leprechaun. Causing mischief, granting wishes, making it sunny.'

'And what do you think?'

'I think... I'm not book smart but I know the land. We're just a bit fortunate and it's a little sunnier than it should be. It rains here fierce enough. I also don't think the leprechaun legend is old enough for those woods. They also don't prey on our desires. Or control animals.'

'Why can't you see the village from the road?'

'You've got me there.'

'And the rainbows?' Max asked.

David just shrugged his shoulders again at this. It seemed he didn't have all the answers.

'Luck of the Irish?' Max tried.

'You're good craic, Maxy.'

They both took a drink and Max accepted the science and mythology a little more. 'No. She's just a spirit that's got a taste for us because we let it. Because us humans are never content and always wanting. She might have moved on or died out, but not if she has her lambs. Would a shepherd move his sheep if the grass grew quick enough and the sheep cleaned up their own shite, used a toilet maybe? No, that Lucky's got it pretty good with us saps. Someone wants something, they'll pay a price and Lucky will grant it. Sometimes you won't even know what you paid. That's why people come back here, even some of the supposedly educated ones after they're done learning about a world where you have to work hard to get rewarded. What's a finger for a grand of change? What's a leg for some talent? What's your eyesight for something you'd never have otherwise?' David finished his tea and stood up to stretch. His crying had long since stopped but he hadn't bothered to wipe away the tracks of his tears. 'So, I'll ask you again, Maxy. What did you ask for?'

## 18

David left shortly after Max had recounted his story. The fact that Max hadn't outwardly asked for anything, like you would a traditional wish to Santa, set David on edge and he said he'd need to go and think on it. Max asked if he was worried that Lucky was getting greedy and David didn't reply. He simply said that if the laws were law, Max was owed something for his fingers. David must have seen a twinkle in Max's eye that he wasn't aware of, because the last thing he said was, "Don't you dare."

What was going on? Were these things real? Fairies, elves, whatever an Aos Sí was and even leprechauns? Or was this one of those superstitious villages that couldn't see the woods - Lucky's Woods - through the trees? What was David putting in his barrels of stout? Max's head and stumps of fingers were throbbing like mad. Feeling queasy, he had to go into the bedroom for a lie down after a day that had gone haywire. He'd only been for a fucking stroll in the woods. To add to all this madness, his body was still punishing him with the remnants of a hangover from the night before, which felt like a kick in the teeth, but his body welcomed the horizontal posture. Perhaps dehydration had aided in his fainting, although he felt less embarrassed about that already. If some malevolent and magical deer had snapped his fingers off, he'd a right to feel shaky about it. His immediate respite in laying down was short lived as his mind went weaselling away among the flood of information he'd just been given. Max still had some holes to fill in this puzzle before it made complete sense - let alone believe it. He needed to know everything about these Aos Sí people, because he'd already made up his mind that there would be justice and it was unlikely to be served by local law enforcement if it was the work of fairies.

*Come on now, murdering faires?*

After David said he believed someone had killed Carla, all Max wanted to do was pick up the phone and dial 999, or whatever it was in Ireland, but as soon as he strayed into the supernatural he knew that would be a dead end and this was a *local* problem. Besides, did he owe this to Carla? He'd shut her out. Perhaps if he hadn't, things would be different. She might have moved back to England after her wife died. Was this his task for repentance? Max slipped his good hand into his pocket and drew his phone out to check the signal. As always, it was next to nothing, but short on ideas he unlocked it and headed straight to a search engine. After a few failed attempts of spelling "Aye See" then adding the words *Irish* and *Folklore,* he came across the Aos Sí, which was spelt nothing like he expected it to be. It was slow going with the connection but he persevered. He imagined this was how fast the internet would have been in the fifties – if the internet had been invented then. He read the brief synopsis on the link while it loaded, stopping on the word *supernatural*.

What was he getting himself into? Was he really about to open up that door and fall down an adult-sized rabbit hole into a world where nothing was off limits? A world where vampires stalked the night, ghouls rattled houses and mermaids sank ships? Forty years of absolute mundanity – school, work, marriage, child, and not so much as a creaking floorboard from the other side. Now he stood at the edge of some great secret a bunch of locals had kept to themselves for who knows how long.

The little bar grew and grew on the loading page and oddly enough so did the feeling of excitement in him. Wasn't this really what everyone wanted? A break from monotony? A chance to step through the looking glass, through the paper pages of fantasy, through that high definition screen of boundless Hollywood imagination? Thoughts of Carla's murder were shamefully far off as his mind fantasised about what else might be real, and where the new line of sanity was. His racing mind kept him entertained as the page loaded and when it finally flicked through to the entry, Max had been thinking of witches and wizards.

He scrolled through the page and, although David had left a lot out, it was as David had said, for the most part. A supernatural race that was driven underground. They had their strengths: magical powers and immortality. They had their weaknesses: an aversion to salt or iron and restricted to the woodland in which they dwelled. They appeared secretive from what Max could make out, but what stung was the supposed fact that they should be minding their own business. This particular Aos Sí *wasn't* minding its own business. The entry also alluded to leprechauns and other fairies he had never heard of before. Max finished the entry then began searching through the links and other sites until his battery drained, no doubt from the strain of loading all that data through the worst connection it had ever seen. He tossed the phone aside and closed his eyes to relieve the mental overload he was experiencing, knowing he was succumbing to the lore.

The evidence was there among the hawthorns. He hadn't realised how closely they had diced with danger in bringing Enid here. More than once he came across mentions of "stealing away children" for their own, or as a sacrifice to someone called The Dark One. That confirmed David's story of parents leaving town to keep their children safe. Enid's knowing screams echoed in his ears once again and it sent a shiver coursing through his body. The jury has convened and come to a decision, Your Honour. Max Vogel believed in fairies.

## 19

Max kept his bandages fresh and his painkillers topped up for the next few days. His body may have replenished the little blood he had lost, but the stubs began to throb in a syncopated beat whenever his heart thumped too heavy. That happened quite often as he kept busy with the main reason any of this had happened in the first place: clearing out Carla's house.

He had been surprised at the efficiency of his work given the circumstances but the mundane task was just what he needed – keep here, donate there, crap in the bag. Dare he say it, he was oddly having a good time.

*You're going mad, that's what this feeling is.*

Regardless, it did little to stifle the fire of retribution that was burning inside him. Each sentimental piece he turned over in his good hand only served to fan the flames inside. He regularly had to pull himself out of a daydream that consisted of him killing an elf-like figure in a myriad of gruesome ways. He sometimes took out his anger on an unfortunate pillow with the poker from the fireside. The first time he picked the poker up, Max appreciated the weight and thought it must be iron despite its high polish.

*Iron. The internet said they don't like iron.*

He never took such things the *internet* said at face value, but what else did he have to go off?

He'd been in touch with Nat and Enid over the phone, but video calls were impossible with the signal. He had to firmly talk Nat out of jumping on a plane and coming to visit him, and that was with keeping the fingers a secret. No one understood him better than Nat, but would she really be able to understand this? She was indeed understanding but he detected a tone of hurt in her voice as if she thought he was purposefully avoiding her – which was true, on account of her safety – but maybe she would put it down to grief. Nat, and especially Enid, needed to stay as far away as possible until this was done, or as done as it could be. Thankfully, Nat's parents were on hand to help with the extra childcare and Max could easily make the taxi hours back up.

Aoife stopped by to check on Max and ended up staying for a couple of hours to help out. Max was very conscious of her eyeline but didn't catch her looking down to his hand once. She merely asked how it was, on arrival, and then continued into the bungalow as she had done on the day she gave him a warning. Did she know Max now knew about Lucky? He was unsure what to make of Aoife anymore. What side of the fence was she on? She had of course been the one that advised them – Enid – to leave. Following them through the forest had been something of a heroic act looking back, but since the accident, she had changed.

Perhaps it was common practice not to enquire after

your neighbours for fear it may be reciprocated, but from what he could tell, Aoife had all her digits and all her senses. Had she lost something else? Max had tried to picture little Aoife down in the woods but he struggled to see how such an assertive woman would be in want of anything. Perhaps her assertiveness was a gift from Lucky? She had given Max a long embrace on leaving that felt very much like his mother's hugs, and he couldn't help but melt into her. For a moment, he thought a few tears might escape him.

David on the other hand hadn't stopped by. Towards the end of the third day, Max popped across to knock on his door, but there had been no answer, so he checked in at the pub. Walking by on the other side of the road he saw enough movement through its mottled windows to indicate it was open. After a short loop around the square, and crossing the road for a closer look, he peeked into the topmost panes of glass. He managed to pick out David returning to the bar, likely from one of the tables. Max was sure the pub wasn't the best place to discuss matters of the supernatural. But why hadn't he come over yet?

*I can't do this alone.*

His hand throbbed from the walk uphill so he headed back home.

The woods were still visible in the setting sun as he walked back down. They looked beautiful, despite the horror he knew lived within. He was still struggling with his sanity on that point. The absence of David, someone else to talk to about Lucky, had started to make it feel like a dream again. He looked back down at his hand.

*This isn't a dream.*

Then another thought surfaced.

*Make a wish.*

Unconsciously, Max's mind ran wild.

*Money, fame, fortune, sex, money, money, money.*

He supposed the damage was already done, perhaps if he—

A door snapped shut to his side and Max jolted out of his stupor. He looked round to see a woman walking slowly down the steps of her house.

She reached the bottom then looked up, seemingly to take in the street for the first time, and met Max's eyes. He felt guilty for his thoughts in an instant. Her eyes were sad; they had known heartache. Max didn't know how he knew this but she seemed to nod in defeated acknowledgment, then headed up the hill.

Max looked back at the woods but the darkness within now seemed prevalent. The beauty was gone. He looked back down to his hand once more. Max reflected that at some point, something would need to be done, and most likely it would be a stupid idea.

## 20

By the end of the week, David still hadn't stopped by and Max was not only getting restless, but annoyed. Any knocks on David's door were ignored, even when Max was sure he was in, and the walks up to the pub had become a bit of an evening ritual for him, throbbing hand in tow. Aoife hadn't called again and the nightly broken up phone calls with Nat were becoming unbearable. They had little to chat about yet Max wanted to tell her everything. He was lonely and sensed he was getting cabin fever, not to mention an almighty itch that needed scratching in the form of a trip to the woods with his new friend – the iron fire poker.

After barely eating a mouthful of his dinner, Max cleared up and treated himself to a tipple from Carla's alcohol cupboard. Max wasn't much of a drinker due to his life on the road. No licence, no job, no money. No aficionado, he grabbed the whisky with the highest number on it – he at least knew fifteen years of ageing was a good sign – and it went down easy enough. Two hours later, and an unmeasured amount of whisky gone, he headed up to the pub, adamant on talking to David. When he reached the little square he heard folk music in the air. It got thicker as he approached the pub and by the time he opened the door, he was practically swimming in it.

The little pub was fit to burst, so much so that Max couldn't get a clear view of the bar. A few people clapped his shoulder as he went by. Max had faint recollections of some of the faces from the first time he had visited, but now his eyes were *open*. A lot of hands donned gloves, which was odd for the height of summer, and even in his drunken state it was easy to discern the floppy pieces of fabric most of them had. Some just the tip, others severed right down to the palm. There were eyes glazed over in a blind foggy mist, some solitary, some in pairs. Through the bottom of a pint glass Max saw a mouth with no teeth, was that also the work of Lucky? He suddenly began to feel uncomfortable in this sea of victims, even though he himself shared a scar. His stomach began to turn on its axis, wanting to drag Max back out of the pub and into the safety of the street. Not watching where he was going he clattered into something hard and looked down to find a woman in a wheelchair, a blanket over her lap. But what was under the blanket? He went to apologise but couldn't find his voice, instead knocking over a collection of walking aids that were propped against another table.

'Ooooh, Maxy's had a drink,' a swimming face said.

The whole table laughed wide mouthed and Max clocked more missing teeth and even a tongue that wasn't present. The brashness of these sacrifices was too much; he was scared. A chorus of cheers came from somewhere else in the room and the music picked up a notch. It sounded as though another instrument had joined in, the tempo rising. Max received a few more pats and a few people said words to him but they were lost to the room. Max pressed on towards the bar. He saw a woman ordering drinks with her hands busy in front of her. It wasn't until the server responded with her own hands that he realised they were communicating in sign language.

Last week he wouldn't have thought anything of these things. Perhaps he wouldn't have even realised it, but now he knew. It was undeniable that these people had been to see Lucky. Max's head began to swim in this manifestation of greed.

*Have to get out of here.*

He turned towards the door but more people were piling in. Before he could get a look at their sacrifices, a firm hand wrapped around his bicep. He gave a little scream that was muted under the music. His head nearly flew off its fleshy plinth as he snapped it round to see David.

He guided Max to the side of the bar and through to the back, then pushed him through a loosely hung door into a hall and the music tapered off.

'David what the hell?' Max slurred.

David continued to lead him on and soon they went through another door and into a small empty courtyard filled with barrels, the air stunk of yeast. 'What are you doing here, Maxy?'

Max didn't care much for the heavy handling. Feeling the effects of the whisky, he went on the offensive.

'It's a fucking *public* house isn't it?'

'Only if I say it is.'

'Fuck you, David. Where the hell have you been?'

'Trying to keep things quiet,' he said, looking around.

'Quiet!' Max said, pointing to the pub with his bandaged hand. 'That's quiet?' Max asked, unsure exactly what he was insinuating – it was a Saturday after all.

David took a glance at his hand and seemed to flinch away slightly.

'Oh, I'm sorry. Does this make you feel uncomfortable?' Max said, waving his bandaged hand in front of David's face. He felt the blood slosh against the end of the stubs but bit back the reaction.

'You're drunk,' David said, like he was about to cut someone off at the bar.

'What of it? What else am I meant to be doing, sharpening my spear for an assault? You said you would sort things out.'

'Ah, I said nothing.'

'You've left me to stew in that house and I had to keep convincing myself that this.' He shook his hand again. 'Really happened. Aoife came over and didn't mention a thing, like this is normal.'

'It is normal.'

'It's not fucking normal.'

'It is round here lad.'

'It's not fucking normal, Dave-y.'

'Don't call me Davey.'

'Oh, you think I like being called Maxy all the fucking time? Like a bloody child?'

'Ah, you're drunk Maxy. Go on home.'

Max had never taken a swing at someone in his entire life. Yet, here he was, winding back with what felt like the might of Mount Olympus behind his curled fist.

David saw it coming from a mile away, he could have

lit a cigarette. Instead, he used the time to step aside and let Max sweep through the air an arching hook.

He lost his footing on the beer soaked floor and came crashing down like the drunk he was.

David came around to his side and began to help him up but Max shrugged him off in a hurry. David raised his hands and backed off. They stared at each other in silence while the beer soaked into his shorts and the strum of folk songs continued to float through the air like an inappropriate backing track. David huffed and put his hands on his hips.

'I know I've not done much. I never have. But we've got to be careful. This community,' David said nodding towards the pub, 'they live for the woods, for Lucky. They need it. They're practically cursed with it.'

Max didn't reply.

'Keep yourself parked there. I'll get you some water and then we can chat a bit, but then you get off home.'

David walked back into the pub and let the music out in waves. The tune sounded old. It bounced melodically in a waltz that was no longer common in the twenty-first century. It started to wind around his bones, filling him with—*No!*

Max picked himself up and ran for the gate in the corner, it was open. Striding back down the hill, Max quickly stopped by the house, grabbing the iron poker and the rest of the whisky.

When David came back with the water, he was halfway down the hill.

## 21

The sun crept down behind the forest as dusk settled in. It cast a long shadow into the surrounding fields, extending its reach into the world of humans. Max felt the cool air whirl around him but didn't break his stride, gulping straight from the bottle of whisky for some courage with his wounded hand. He may have missed one swing tonight but he wasn't going to let that stop him – at least that's what the alcohol told him. He gripped the poker tight in his good hand, and its unyielding form filled him with confidence.

He entered the forest on the same path he had before. The light dropped as he proceeded but there was still enough to see where he was going. He slowed as he approached the fork and the site of where the deer had attacked him, but didn't see anything lurking. He came to a complete stop and listened for movement. The chirp of a few birds nesting for the day but nothing on the forest floor. On reaching the next clearing, everything looked as it had before – several paths leading off, but no deer. Max had made it here at quite a pace and his heart was beating to keep up. Looking at each path leading off, Max tried to assess which he should take based on the extent of their use. If it really was a common act to come and make a sacrifice, the signs would be there. For the most part, they all looked well-trodden but there was a slightly wider path that caught his attention. After seeing a hawthorn at its gate he proceeded on. This path was the longest yet. Although wide at first, it narrowed enough to allow the low bramble a go at his exposed legs. Why had he chosen to storm the woods in shorts and a polo shirt? After another few stops to check for sounds, Max wasn't too sure if the path would lead to another clearing, but then something spoke.

'You left before I could return the favour.'

Max wanted to search for the source of the sound but he was frozen with fear; it had come from all around him.

*Fuck. You really thought this was a good idea?*

The voice was delicate but it resonated with the force of something much bigger, Max struggled to stifle the chill that tore up his spine. Any slither of doubt he had left evaporated. This wasn't some local superstition. Lucky was real.

'Lucky?'

'Do you really need an answer?' Again the sound of the voice surrounded him. 'You've brought a little toy with you. Is that for me?'

'It is,' Max said, trying to sound like a hero, but without anything to strike at, his confidence began to seep away. The poker felt heavier than it had on the way in. He raised it up like a sword but it felt more like a useless and heavy umbrella.

'Very kind, but I have no need for such things. Besides, it is *I* that has a gift for you. What is your wish?'

'I don't want your wishes. I didn't ask for anything. You took my fucking fingers for fun.'

'Didn't ask?' Lucky questioned. 'But your heart asks for many things. Do you not hear it?'

'I didn't ask for anything,' he repeated.

'Then do you wish for them back?'

'What?'

'Your fingers. Would you like them back, is that your wish? It's quite a reasonable request for the sacrifice, tit for tat,'

'No I don't want your fucking fingers,' Max said, not wanting to give Lucky the satisfaction of a granted wish.

'Well, yes, I suppose they are mine, but if I return them to you they will be yours again.'

'Stop fucking playing with me, Lucky. I'm not an idiot like the rest of those villagers.'

'Come now. Such harsh words. You barely know these people, and you should not assume to know things that you do not understand.'

Max pivoted on the spot with the poker raised.

'For example, you assume I am afraid of that poker. Have you been reading about such things in children's books? Going to strike me down with iron?'

Max shifted his grip on the poker and began swaying it, calling Lucky's bluff. 'Well, you're not showing yourself, are you?'

'And why should I waste time with you when you don't even respect the laws at play here?'

'Because you murdered my sister! What fucking laws are you respecting?' Max didn't get a reply to this and continued to pivot.

The dusk looked to be short-lived and fear of losing his way back and getting stuck in this haunted place added to his haste to be done with this. He felt his normal navigational talent wouldn't work in this place.

Finally, Lucky spoke, and this time Max was able to pinpoint a source. It was close. He turned to face its direction and felt his bowels rumble. It was the deer that had taken his fingers. The light was low, yet the deer seemed to be emitting its own light. The side of its head remained bloody and caved, a slithering mess of maggots burrowing in and out, the buzz of their hatched lava vibrating the air.

'I respected the laws and your sister paid the price for her wish.' The voice, although clearly emanating from the deer, was still disembodied, as the deer's mouth stayed shut. Just the tear on its snout showed that gruesome row of shattered teeth.

In his fear, Max took a step back rather than striking the deer, but kept the iron poker raised.

'No wish is worth a life,' he said.

'It is when you've nothing left to give. Your sister was somewhat devoid of care for her own wellbeing. Blindness would not have paid the price, nor a finger or two. I merely planted the disease. Your sister was too weak to fight it.'

The realisation of his sister's fate struck Max hard. So it was Lucky. David was right. Disease or not, Lucky had set the wheels in motion and she needed to pay.

'Are you not curious to know what she asked for?'

'What?' Max asked, completely uninterested in his

sister's dying wish. All he wanted was to kill this deer, although he wasn't totally sure if this *was* Lucky or just one of her pawns.

'She wished for you, Max. She wished for her own flesh and blood to come to Ireland and forgive her.'

## 22

---

Max felt as if his severed stubs had opened up again and his blood was pouring out of them. Was this true? Did Lucky really have the power to do that?

*That's why I came?*

It's true that Max never answered the phone to Ireland but something had taken on him to pick it up that morning. But it was all too late. Whatever Lucky had planted in Carla had grown and devoured her in a matter of days. Lucky had tricked Carla. She'd read between the lines in her sick way, knowing her death would be the only way to get Max here and ultimately forgive her. Wish granted.

'And here you are,' Lucky said, as if reading his thoughts and awaiting an applause from an unseen audience. Max didn't care much for the clarification, he was the evidence after all. If this was true... it was all his fault.

*She's dead because of me.*

'So tell me, Max. Who really killed your sister?' Lucky said.

Not knowing what else to do, Max found some resolve and revolved the poker so that it now resembled an oversized dagger. He wanted to feel the jagged tip tear through the broken flesh of the deer. He wanted to finish off the job that Aoife's jeep had started and stab and stab and stab. He strode forward, raised the poker and brought it down into the side of the deer's head. It went through like butter, all the way up to his hand. He felt the mix of blood, gristle and maggots splash his hand, but the blood was cold.

*It's all so cold.*

The deer didn't go down and Max panicked it might snap at him. He retracted the poker with a disgusting squelch and thought he was going to lose his stomach. Instead, he came down again and again and again, just as planned. Although, he didn't feel the satisfaction he had dreamed of in any of the strikes.

After what must have been half a dozen strikes he left the poker in the deer's head, its polished tip protruding out the other side. He stepped back and flicked his hand through the air to try and shake off the cocktail of deer and maggots, his breath gone. The deer's head had slightly yielded with each blow but otherwise it stood strong like the trees that surrounded it.

Then it took a powerful step forward and Max really did let his bowels go. He didn't know what he had gotten himself into but he was quite sure this was the end. It was only a matter of time until one of them did something stupid and it looked like he'd beaten David to it. Here he stood alone, miles away from home, far from his soon-to-be widow, far from his soon to be fatherless child, with his own shit running down his legs. Better than someone else's shit, the drunken part of him thought. He closed his eyes and sobbed. Max wasn't sure how Lucky and her valiant deer would go about killing him, but he heard it before he felt it. Two sharp cracks filled the dusk air, resonating around the forest like gunshots and the right side of his body filled with fire.

*My god, she's burning me alive with her magic!*

Then there was a loud thud and a voice.

'Maxy!' There were only two people who called him that and right now he didn't give a shit how it sounded. He'd happily get it tattooed on his forehead for what it was worth.

Max opened his eyes with a flinch. The deer had gone. He looked around and just about made out David cutting through the woodland towards him, he had a shotgun broken over his arm and was reloading it with two fresh cartridges.

'I—'

'Are you ok?' David asked.

Unsure what to say, Max just started crying.

'Alright, alright lad.'

'Lucky,' Max managed to say.

'Yeah, yeah. I heard the bitch.' David hacked some phlegm and spat where the deer had been.

Max looked down and saw the deer dead on its side. It may have already been dead but now it was double dead. It's entire body was streaked with moving embers like it was made of paper and had been set alight. There was a perceptible sizzle and Max was mesmerised at the sight, watching the way embers joined and proceeded across the body, devouring the deer and leaving behind a coal-like substance.

'Come on, we don't have long,' David said, clicking his shotgun back together. 'She'll be back with another pawn.'

'But—' Max looked back down at the deer.

'No time to explain now, move it.'

And so they left at a pace, Max following David through the forest until they reached a path, and before long they were out into a field. Max could just make out the road in the dying light. It didn't even look as if he'd gone as deep as it had felt.

'Next time,' David said with a smile on his face. 'You might want to try using a naked iron poker. Carla's was chrome plated you eejit.'

# 23

Max stood in the shower letting the warm water massage the right side of his body. Although David had hit the deer clean for the most part, Max's forearm and calf had caught some of the spray, which consisted of hot rock salt. David said he would explain later and asked him to clean up, promising this time he would return after closing down the pub. "Got to keep up appearances" he had said.

After David had saved Max's life, Max didn't have any issues with him disappearing again. In truth, he needed some time to shake off the fear that had smothered him in the forest. He had thought it was the end of the line for him. How could he have been so stupid? He had Nat and Enid to think about. But had he really believed it all?

*If you need any more convincing, you will get yourself killed.*

His sanity was cracking but still seemed to be intact. After the shower, he got into some fresh clothes, opting for longer length jeans this time, and put the kettle on. Any feeling from the whisky he'd drunk had amazingly left his body, his visceral fear giving it a solid boot. He wouldn't be drinking again. Ever. Max headed to the armchair and picked up the pillow that had served as target practice for the poker. What a waste of time that had been.

'Firing blanks,' he said to himself, taking a seat and holding the pillow close for comfort. He'd just taken his first sip of tea when there was a knock on the door and he choked the mouthful down.

*Was that David, already? Why hadn't he come through the back? Shit, was the back door unlocked, what if Lucky came in that way, what if it was another deer hoofing at the door?*

Max wanted to crawl into the fabric of the armchair; his nerves were shot.

'Max? It's David.'

Max released a breath he didn't know he was holding and headed for the door but he stopped short of opening it and called out.

'David?'

'Yes, it's David.' It sure sounded like David, but Max couldn't bring himself to open the door. What if it was a trick? 'Max?' said David's voice again. Max didn't reply.

*Why wasn't he calling him Maxy?*

David spoke again, but this time Max could sense him pressed right on the other side of the door.

'She can't leave the woods. Aos Sí don't wander far. You're safe.'

*That's exactly what Lucky would say.*

'Sure, it's just…' Max started.

'What?' David said.

'What's my name?'

'What are you on about, lad?'

'What's my name?' he repeated.

'Max... I don't know your feckin' last name. Is it Vogel too?'

'Yes.'

*Shit. Don't give it away.*

'Maxy. Your name is Maxy. Is that the feckin problem here? I'm trying not to wind you up. You took a swing at me earlier. Landed on your arse. Is that proof enough for you that it's me? I know you're rattled, but open this door you tool.'

Max had forgotten about that, the situation came swimming into view again through a drunken lens. Lucky hadn't been in the pub courtyard and that was David's blunt manner all right. Max opened the door but still sighed relief at the sight of David. He closed the door as soon as David had crossed the threshold, without a look to the outside world, where *she* lived.

'Ah Jesus. You look like shite,' David said. 'Do we need to go to the hospital again?'

'I had a shower,' Max said in his defence. David didn't look convinced.

'Can I get you one?' Max offered, motioning to his tea.

'No, you're alright. I won't stay long.'

'Thank you,' Max said. 'For earlier. I don't think I said it. But thank you.'

David gave a series of nods and Max felt that they now shared a bond that would last a lifetime, however long that might end up being. David dug into his pockets and removed some small bright red cylinders. The light caught a brass cap which topped one end and Max realised they were shotgun shells.

'This is what I was busying myself with.' David took

one and placed it in Max's hand. Having never handled guns or ammunition before, Max wasn't sure what to make of it. He went to give it a shake but then realising it was a ballistic object thought better of it. He didn't know how these things worked and didn't want to lose any more fingers.

'Is it different from normal ones?'

'It is. I loaded it with rock salt. That's why I said to shower, I caught you in the blast. It wasn't just the...' David looked a bit embarrassed, 'you know.'

'Sorry about that,' Max said.

David waved him off.

'And sorry about the swing,' Max added.

'Ah, it's fine. I can be an arse.'

'So. They don't like salt, the Aos Sí?'

'Honestly, it was a hunch. I spray salt water around when I go in, something our grandparents used to say about fairies. Lead either doesn't affect her or she could tell that it was chrome plated. I don't know how it works. I only go in for the hazelnuts. My one vice. Either way, she minds her business and I mind mine. Well. I did.' David looked at Max and seemed to take him in for the first time. 'I'm sorry, I know all this is a shock. You've got to understand something Max, and it's very important that you do: no one around here wants Lucky dead. Not even those that don't use her, few as they are. They'll think it's bad luck or some shite. They'd never dream of killing her and they wouldn't even be caught thinking it.'

'Do you think she's got them under some kind of spell?' A few days ago a question like that would have only been figurative, Max now realised he was talking literally.

'No spell needed. Just a bunch of greedy human gobshites. Maybe it's the trill, some sick punishment fetish this lot have got. You saw Glenn the other night, he was bouncing when he walked in. Those aren't the only fingers he's lost, let me tell you. He likes it, I can tell. They get used to it. I know you had your... moment after your fingers went, but you didn't know, did you?' David looked around the room that Max was sorting. 'You've been awfully productive have you not? You were up, now you're coming down.'

'But how—'

'I don't know for sure. I just hear things, see things. Attitudes change. I've got good at telling. Part of the reason I was avoiding you in truth, I didn't want to know if you'd be affected. Once you know, it might be addictive for all I know. Would explain some things. Ah Jesus, I shouldn't be telling you this. Don't you dare go making wishes Max. That's exactly what she wants. Then you're hooked. Don't forget what happened to Carla. That was Lucky's doing, even if she didn't pull the trigger. It was her gun, her bullet.'

Max nodded, unable to believe that anyone could be so stupid to go back to Lucky. But what had he felt the other night at the top of the hill? Something was calling him to make a wish. Maybe he wasn't so smart, or maybe it wasn't that stupid. David might not want to say it out loud, but it certainly sounded like magic to Max.

'So, you've never been to see Lucky? How do you know so much about her?'

'I said, I hear, I see. Then there's also our "training" At least that's what I think of it as now. My grandparents used to tell tales when they'd visit us out of town. I think they all do in this community. Just harmless fairy tales, but really they're just warming you up so you don't get a complete shock if you move back. Look at you. Clearly this is what happens if you're not *warmed up.* You near lost your mind going in there like that. These aren't fairy tales.'

'Fairy tales,' Max repeated uselessly.

'Yup, and there's truth in some of it lad. Also, you forget I run a pub. A pub where most visit Lucky when they need something, and drink makes for flappy gums.'

'And you've never—' Max started but David cut him off vehemently.

'I'd never give her the satisfaction. I may not be smart-smart but I learn from what I overhear. People are more chatty with others who visit her. It's like a sick little club. But your sister…' David trailed off.

'Go on.'

'Well, your sister talked to me. After her wife passed, she felt alone here, like it was never really her home. She was too smart for this place in truth. She felt trapped.'

## 24

David tapered off after he mentioned Carla being trapped and, although still not understanding what their relationship had been, Max didn't want to pry. He didn't have the energy to delve into now, as selfish as it was. His adrenaline had scarpered. All he longed for was bed. Seeing this, David was polite enough to take his leave.

'Don't you go fretting about Lucky. She'll stay where she is. Rest up and we'll have a proper chat tomorrow lad.'

'Thank you. I mean that.' Max said.

David looked deep into Max's eyes. Perhaps he saw a trace of his sister's hazel tones in there as he seemed to not manage it for too long and headed for the door. 'I'll see you in the morning. Not sure when, but I won't keep you in the dark again. Can't have you going John Rambo with a salt shaker next time.' Max appreciated that even after the evening's events, David was able to keep joking. His gratitude was bottomless.

'And I'm sorry again for taking a swing,'

'And I'm sorry you're a lousy shot,' David smiled back. 'Goodnight, *Max.*'

'Goodnight.'

Max locked up and, despite what David had said about Lucky being bound to the forest, he pushed one of Carla's dining chairs up against the front door. The back was a bit more problematic with the bifold doors and all Max could do was pull the curtains to stop his mind from seeing things. He stood in the empty room. The silence was uncomfortable. Perhaps he should put a record on?

*And find another drawing?*

No, perhaps he should get himself to bed. He gave the room a final cautious sweep with his eyes before leaving and they came to rest on the polished tools by the fireplace.

'You idiot,' he said to himself. It did strike him that he should take *some* protection to the bedroom to help him sleep – the adult equivalent of a child and their teddy bear.

*She can't leave the woods.*

'Yeah, and fairies don't exist.' Not confident that raw iron would do the trick, even if he had it, he headed to the kitchen and picked up the box of salt he and Nat had brought on the way here – Max didn't tend to holiday without it for fear of bland meals. It didn't carry the reassuring weight of the poker but at least he knew it would work. Leaving the room, he brushed the counter with his arm and his pain receptors reminded him of the rock salt shrapnel. Between this on his right side, and his useless hand on his left, he felt even more vulnerable. What if he missed? He retrieved the biggest glass he could find and filled it with salt and water. He gave it a stir to dilute it and thought that would be a good backup. Would that be enough? He took down more glasses one by one, filled them with salt and added water to some. He carried them to the bedroom, shut the door, wedged another chair against it and got into bed. He only told himself once that he was being silly but he was quick to shut this down, now acknowledging that he lived in a world of supernatural beings. Max got into bed and his exhaustion was enough to send him off.

Hours later, Max found himself in a forest and instantly he was lucid in the dream, or soon to be nightmare more likely. Max wasn't a stranger to such things and any minute now he'd get a little surge of adrenaline and it would wake him up. Only this time, he didn't. He tried to blink his eyes open but they felt heavy. Tucked safely away in his sister's spare bed his eyes gave a little flicker. It was hard to place exactly, but he gathered this was his mind's manifestation of Lucky's Woods. The sun was shining and a breeze pulled through the thicket but there was no noise. He was surrounded by a mix of trees but beyond that it became foggy, as if his mind hadn't bothered to render the finer details, instead opting for a light mist. Suddenly, the right side of his peripheral vision caught movement and he stumbled around to face it.

Walking away from him, seemingly uninterested in his presence, was a naked woman. Her hair was short, loosely curled and wild. It bounced gently at the nape of her neck as she walked. The skin on her back shimmered like the iridescent shell of a beetle as it caught the rays of light breaking through the canopy above. It seamlessly blended into skin again as it reached her coccyx, and Max felt heat rise in his cheeks as his eyes glazed over *her* cheeks. His eyes were drawn down to just below her knee where a deep moss had grown, giving the appearance of well-fitted green wellies. She was just reaching the mist line and Max thought she was going to disappear, but then all of a sudden he began to move not to her, but with her.

He looked down at the forest floor and panic set in as he saw it was alive and carrying him forwards. Leaves and twigs washed over each other in a silent wave while insects, too abundant to count, surfaced and dove into the mulch like dolphins in an ocean. He tried to jump off Mother Nature's surfboard, but wherever he placed a foot, a new wave appeared, carrying him onwards towards the woman. He turned and tried to run in the other direction but he might as well have been running on a treadmill. He turned once more to face the woman again and saw she had stopped near an opening which led onto a road, but Max kept on moving. *Now* he was getting closer. He tried to dig in with his heels but the waves kept on and he lost his footing, falling backwards to the ground with a bushy thump. The waves were all around him now, breaking, crashing, carrying him on. He tried to get back up but the insects were crawling over his hands and legs, and soon the leaves followed in their wake. He was sinking.

He felt a tug at his wrists and was horrified to see that vines were now wrapping around his limps, restraining him and pulling him flat onto his back. Still, he moved onwards towards the woman. The leafy waves began splashing his mouth. Rotting, damp forest floor filled his mouth and just before he reached the woman's mossy wellies, his adrenaline upped its dosage and he awoke.

He felt the dampness in the sheets from his sweat but lay dead still in the dark bedroom like a petrified child, even though somehow he now *unquestionably* knew that Lucky could not leave her forest, her *woods*. Lucky's Woods. She was waiting for something.

Max stayed there until the sun came up and the birds started chirping.

## 25

After another quick security check at the door – "You hate being called Maxy" – Max let David in. One quick look at David's face told Max all he needed to know. The shadows were there from a bad night's sleep, the eyelids a little lower than normal, and although he was afraid of the answer, he asked anyway.

'Did you… dream of her?'

'If you want to call it a dream.' David headed on through to the living area as usual. It seemed David and Aoife had been to Carla's a lot, as both made themselves feel at home without Max's invitation.

'Well, yes. But what was it? I was lucid straight away,' he said, following in David's wake.

'Ah, stop with your fancy words.'

'I knew I was dreaming. That it wasn't real,' Max explained.

David nodded in understanding, but there was something else.

'I don't think that was a dream,' David said.

'No?' Max said, thinking. 'No, I think you're probably right. But what? A vision, a premonition?'

'I think she was trying to put the shits up us. Plain and simple. Payback for finishing that deer off. We cost her a pawn.' Was Lucky really that petulant?

'What did you see?' Max asked, watching David fight off a shiver at the question.

'Woods. Or *forest*, whatever you want. Looked like Lucky's Woods, but misty. I've never seen it like that before. Then I saw Lucky – I guess it was her – from behind. Not wearing much of anything mind. And then...' David shivered again, 'forest floor was moving and pulling me forward towards that bitch.'

'And then you went under?'

'Under what?'

'The forest pulled you under, into the ground?' Max said, embarrassed. Had David not suffered the same leafy doom? Was he yet again the damsel in the story?

David shook his head. 'No, it took me up behind her, near a road. It was all silent but I think I heard a car coming. Road noise.'

'Who was in the car?'

'Ah, I didn't get that far,' David smirked. 'I took a swing at her from behind and then I woke up. As good as throwing punches as you. I just wanted to make her pay for what she did to Carla. I don't care what she does to those other dopes, they ask for it. But what she did. It's not right; she overstepped the mark.'

'Did she suffer?' Max asked, he didn't know what brought it on but he suddenly needed to know. 'Carla?'

David looked up, sadness now pushing aside the tiredness. They hadn't had a chance to speak about this since they had found out Lucky had planted the seed that eventually killed her.

'Carla was strong, always was. I heard Lucky talking to you, saying Carla had nothing left in her, but that's a feckin' lie. She had a lot in her, I saw it. I was lucky enough to feel it. Those couple days at the end when she stopped gardening, that wasn't her feeling low. That was Lucky's disease eating away at her. If she was suffering, it was in silence. She never said so. I saw her sitting at the back of the garden. She was just sketching and sketching. But it was quick – two days. Mercy that it is.' David was blunt as a brick but it was undeniable that he had loved Carla perhaps more than anyone knew.

Max went into the kitchen for a tissue but David shrugged it off saying he was ok.

'So, now we've seen her, we definitely know it's a person, of sorts,' Max said, trying to move it on and spare David any further pain.

'And a show off at that, walking around in the nude. Who does she think she is?'

'I guess it's her home after all,' Max said, thinking about how he walked around naked back in Furlong.

*Ah, Furlong.*

What he wouldn't give to be in boring, normal old Furlong. David interrupted his daydream before he could indulge further.

'Are you defending her, so?'

'What? No, I'm just. Never mind. I was wondering about the deer though.'

'Yeah, that's just her magic. My grandparents went on about that one a lot when they visited. Kids like animals so it's a woolly place to start. She tames them, or puts a spell on them or something. They're just toys to her. But what she did to that deer, keeping it alive. Well, let's just say my grandparents left out that part.'

'Zombie animals.'

'Ah, don't say that word. Ain't we got enough supernatural shite to be dealing with? Thought I knew the guts of it, then here we are talking about a shared vision and deer that don't know when to die.'

Max had automatically stuck the kettle on while in the kitchen, even though he didn't want a hot drink, he motioned to David who nodded. The sound filled the silence and he thought more about the dream as he watched the bubbles rise through the glass casing. He'd never drunk so much tea but it gave him something to do and did keep him calm.

'Max,' David said seriously, when he brought the tea over, 'I know I said this last night but you really have to understand that this thing that we call Lucky, she's not here to grant wishes. Sure, that's how people see it. But she's evil.'

'Malevolent not benevolent.' Max said.

'Are you trying to take the piss now, college boy? How many times—'

'No, sorry. It's something I read. When I was trying to suss out the Aos Sí. Said that some are just plain mean. Hold a grudge for being driven underground,' Max said.

David nodded in agreement. 'She gets off on that kind of thing. She doesn't take fingers because she's hungry, it's not like that. She does the things she does because she can and she thinks it's a gas. She grants wishes because she enjoys taking from people, because all they ask for are trivial things. Ninety nine percent of the time it's just people asking for shite, I bet you. It's like this village was put here just for her craic. We're her little flock of sheep.'

'So, what do we do?'

'Do? Nothing lad. We can rub ourselves in salt and go rolling into those woods with a tank, but unless we actually get to that geebag it's pointless. I don't think it'll do anything to just kill the animals under her control. She'll just get more and then send us another vision as a present.'

'So we need to tempt her out? Or find out where she actually hides in there? I read something about hawthorns and how the Aos Sí value them.'

'Tempt her out? Max, I don't think you're hearing me. I'm furious, beyond it, for what she did to Carla, but—'

'Maybe if we can find where she lives in the forest?'

'Max. Stop.'

'It can't be hard to find her. Everyone else does.'

'They might be talking to feckin' squirrels for all we know. I know the *woods* but I don't go down there unless I can help it. And you shouldn't either.'

'Surely someone knows them well? How about that Glenn? He had fingers off.'

'Hah. Man's a drunk and couldn't find north with a compass. Besides, I told you this has got to stay between us, and even then we're fools to try something. No one wants that thing dead and if it gets out that we're after it…' David didn't finish but Max could quite easily see everyone coming down on them. It seemed like the community really was under a spell.

'I don't want to leave this David. She's got to pay for what she did.'

David looked at Max, choosing his words. 'I know it's

not my place, Max. But it's hard to hear you say that as if *now* you care. All the years Carla wanted to see you, you never came. She even flew back to England that time.'

Max thought he was going to take another swing at David and this time he wasn't even drunk. The fire quickly went out when his conscience poured a bucket of guilt over it. He had no words. He wasn't even sure what David or anyone around here knew about their relationship, what Carla had told them. Max was in the wrong when it came to their relationship.

'She didn't even know you had a child, did she?'

'No. How did you—'

'Because she wouldn't have made that wish if she did. She wouldn't have risked putting her own niece in danger. That wasn't Carla.'

*This is all my fault.*

'Ah, you know what lad, forget what I said. It's not my business,' David said, briskly finishing his drink off and getting up to leave.

'No it's fine. You're right. I was a shit brother. Awful. You were actually here for Carla at the end. I wasn't. You're owed an explanation. It's stupid, it really is.' The past twenty three years flew by Max's eyes in a second and he had to move across to the armchair that had served him well in the last week for support. He finished his own tea and went on.

———

'At its core, we grew apart, but it was me who had the growth spurt. Our dad passed away young, fifty-three. Brain haemorrhage, while induced for some kidney infection. On my birthday no less, I had just turned seventeen. Carla was nearly thirty, not living at home but we were still close. We used to listen to records together, even though CDs had mostly taken over by then. She knew what bands to follow and who was still pressing. She should have been a DJ really.' Max pointed to the vinyl he was planning to take with him. 'I was there for a lot of those purchases.'

'Carla listened to them a lot,' David said. A lump rose in Max's throat at the thought of her sitting alone listening to the records they had once shared. He composed himself and pressed on.

'We saw less of each other after my father passed. One less birthday to attend, one less obligatory Father's Day lunch. Our mother's house still served as the round table and the offer was always open to visit. I had just got my driving licence and practically lived in my car. It was an escape for me; I didn't really mourn. I hadn't just got the keys to a car, it was a key to the country, to freedom. I was all over the place. Carla moved to Dublin the same year, and that was fine you know, why shouldn't she? No need to hang around for me. We've always been at different stages in our life – she was eight years older.'

'Big gap,' David said. He was clearly trying to save Max the pain after having asked such an outright question. But Max knew he should air it out and appreciated David's support.

'Yeah. My parents struggled to get pregnant after they had Carla. I guess they never thought it would happen in the end, so they stopped taking precautions. Then I popped out eight years later. So, we'd been speaking less and less, barely saw each other, and eventually it took our mother's death to bring us together again. She made it to seventy, but it's still young. Apparently Vogels aren't ones for sticking around. I can't imagine going in another thirty odd years. That's too soon. Isn't it?'

David nodded politely.

'So, she flew over for the funeral and we had an argument.' Max shook his head at the nonsense of it all.

'What about?'

'Money, of course. Isn't everything about money? The petty amount that our parents had left us, selling the house, pensions. Stupid looking back. We told each other to fuck off and we never really patched it up. The gap just widened over the years. So, there she was in Ireland with her wife, I was in England married and well into my own life. I dunno. Normally these things just heal themselves but somehow this didn't. Perhaps it was the distance. We didn't talk as such but she invited me to Ireland a few times, clearly wanting to sort it out face to face. I said no then stopped replying. Each time I ignored her it just made it harder for me to reach out. Pride. When she flew over I said I was too busy to see her. My own sister. I had to tell Nat not to open the door when she actually came to our house. Imagine that. It's like that life was dead for me and for some reason I was glad of it, glad to not have to worry about anyone else but Nat. We'd been trying for a child for a long time, and it seemed that we'd picked up the same luck as my parents. I was beyond stress and I didn't need more reminding of my parents and their troubles with me. Carla wasn't that mad about it though, I think. She left a nice voice message and what do I do?' Max said, wanting David to finish the story so he wouldn't need to taste the words in his own mouth.

David only returned a kind shrug.

'I told her to stop phoning me. Stop contacting me.' Max was struggling for breath now. How could he have been so bitter, so obtuse? They would have made up in a second had they seen each other, he knew it. Why hadn't he allowed it? Pride. Why had he let it go on for so long and stagnate into this mess? Pride. Did that make him any better than the locals here? He looked down at his bandaged hand.

'I've been thinking a lot on it. It's not an excuse, but I think it all stems from our dad. I didn't deal with that well, which made our mum's passing worse. Perhaps I thought if I distanced myself from Carla, I wouldn't have to feel that kind of pain again.' Max's vision swam with tears and they finally broke the levy. 'My god. I killed her David. If I'd just opened the door, answered the fucking phone, stayed in touch... she would never have made that wish. I have to make this right. Maybe it's selfish, maybe I need this to quench my own guilt. I know it won't bring her back, but Lucky's got to pay, hasn't she?'

'Of course she does. Of course she does,' David said. Max knew how petty he looked to David. He didn't really have a blinding resumé as a brother, and his recent antics hadn't been any better. 'But Max, she didn't know that her wish would kill her. Lucky overstepped the mark.'

'Are you sure she didn't know?'

'Well, not certain but...' David started, then instead found it more important to give his hair a ruffle.

'What?'

'Lucky doesn't tell you what she's going to take. Sometimes she takes it when you're not looking. She's acting the maggot. I said she just likes toying with us humans, makes you think you got off light. I was getting a lift one day with Sara – used to work with me at the pub. She'd just got herself a brand new Range Rover. You can guess where that money came from. There we were, driving out near Galway for some supplies, and she goes blind. Just like that.'

'Fuck.'

'Fuck indeed. Sent it into a shop front, screaming. Try explaining that one to the police: "She wasn't blind when she got in the car, officer."'

'Was she not angry?'

'See, you've got your head on straight Max,' David said, slapping the tabletop. 'I asked her if she thought it was right, what Lucky did to her. But they get all funny, like it's blasphemy to question her ways. They're all sick. Carla's always lived a modest life and I would never have put her down asking for riches or anything.'

Max looked at the box of vinyl as David finished off and then it all became clear.

'Messages. David. Maybe she knew when she got really sick that it was Lucky. Look.' Max went across to the vinyl and began pulling out the ones he remembered purchasing with her. 'The drawing you saw the other night, that was in the first record we bought together and I bet...' Max looked for another record they'd bought together and found *Damn The Torpedoes* by Tom Petty and the Heartbreakers. What a find that had been.

'What?' David said, coming over.

Max popped the sleeve and felt that all too familiar chill rise through his body again.

'Fuck me.'

## 26

---

'Look,' David said, pointing to the base of a very large hawthorn tree in bloom. It was almost comically large for the species. With just a pencil, Carla had managed to depict the little flowers perfectly with her expert strokes. It gave the impression of a tree covered in cotton. Max wanted to reach out and feel her delicate work under his fingers, but what David had pointed out made him wary. The gnarled roots of the tree were exposed as if they had been well trodden, causing the soil to fall away, and between the largest of these two woody legs was what looked like an entrance to a burrow, a very large burrow. Carla's pencil had taken a bit of a turn here. Whereas everything else was perfectly shaded in one direction, this was a complete mess. Her pencil had run side to side, up and down and round and round like a toddler's first masterpiece. The lines had breached their walls causing the deep grey darkness to spread as if it was reaching out and consuming more than it should. There was nothing else on the page. Just a portrait of the beautiful tree and its menacing hole, everything else was white.

'That's her den,' Max said.

'Well. They say the Aos Sí were driven underground by us humans. But I never really thought it meant *under-the-ground*. More like an underground community.'

'Maybe it really is underground. Maybe they use gateways like this to get there?'

'Ah, Jesus. I don't know.'

'Does this exact tree exist?'

'I've never seen it,' David finished, with an unconscious shiver that said he'd never wish to.

'I think Carla wanted me to find it. She wanted to let me know she'd been tricked. That's why there are pictures in the vinyl. She knew I'd go looking through them. I just don't know why she didn't spell it out for me.' Max reflected on the events of the past week. Would he really have believed his sister? A sister that he hadn't seen in years? Even if she had spelt it out for him? He would have thought she'd gone senile in this little community. 'Maybe she wanted me to find out about Lucky myself. We both enjoyed nature because of our father and she knew this would pull me in. There must be someone who knows, David. Please.'

'Max, I want to make her pay as much as you do, but what chance do we really have against that supernatural thing? Look at the damage Lucky did with a deer. Carla wasn't thinking straight *if* she was trying to tell you. Maybe the cancer… I'm just starting to think it's better we leave this—'

'Leave it?' Max said. 'I can't leave it and I know you can't leave it either. What's all that about *loving* my sister?

You seemed to gloss over that fact every time, like I should have known that you love her. Does everyone else know?'

David pulled back from the picture they were studying. 'I told you, it's all private here.'

'Oh, bullshit David. We always end up arguing and it's because you're too tight to open up. If you really loved her, you'd help.'

'Don't you feckin' start lad. I did love her,' he said, his eyes glistening with memories that Max didn't know. 'And I still love her.'

Max instantly regretted pushing David. 'I'm sorry, David. I'm… well, I'm a fucking dick aren't I? You know the story now.'

David paced around and composed himself. 'We're just two fleshy pieces of meat, Max. Lucky has been around for thousands of years. I think I've been kidding myself. I would have done something sooner if I really thought I could,'

'But, maybe together we can. You'd at least do some asking around. What's the harm in that?'

'Are you deaf, so? You are pushing it. Lucky's going to be the least of our worries if I do that. These chancers are feral about their special relationship with Lucky. They'll kill us and feed us to the birds. No one will ever find out. They'll wish away any nuisance or attention. They won't think twice about a sacrifice to keep up this circus.'

Max knew he was putting David in an impossible position, but he had to press on. Recounting the story of Carla and their relationship had only served to show what an idiot Max had been. Her death was on his hands no matter what David said.

'Well,' Max started, cautiously, not wanting to lose the battle, 'what if we ask the right people? What about Aoife?'

'Ah Jesus. I see where you're going but—'

'She's safe to talk to, I know it. She warned me about Enid and sent us packing. She followed us through the woods, she drove us on when I was going to stop. She knew, David! She knew that Lucky would try something. She must know Lucky well enough.'

'Your little pup?' David said. 'It could have riled Lucky up, sure. But that doesn't mean Aoife knows more. People have always been smart enough to leave the moment they know they're pregnant, it's like we evolved to learn that. They'll always have a home here, Aoife does all the paperwork for it. A little wish to Lucky from the other half is all you need to tide things over until it's safe to come back. It could have been forever since Lucky's had a kid around. But we've never really known the danger because we get out.' David walked over to the back door and looked out. 'Aoife's smart is all. Not everyone uses Lucky. I wouldn't have Aoife down for one, she—'

Max had already left his seat and headed for the door.

## 27

Aoife opened the door after the second knock. At first, she looked furious at being disturbed, but on seeing Max on her doorstep with David chasing not far behind, it turned to worry. She looked back over her shoulder then came off the step and close to them.

'Five minutes,' she said. 'You both bugger off then come back in five minutes.'

Max waited for a protest from David behind but there was none.

'And don't be getting yourselves seen. I mean that.'

They both returned to David's silently.

'You're lucky lad. Aoife seems to be soft on you.'

'We'll see. I'm about to ruin my image.'

From the upstairs window they watched as they saw a man and a woman leave who David identified as Mr. and Ms. Walsh. They waited a bit longer, then returned to Aoife's. This time she opened before Max's knuckles reached the door.

'In!' she snapped and pointed.

They darted in and she shut the door in such a rush she slammed into David's shoulder.

'Argh, watch it!' he said.

'Oh, David!' she said, with a hand to her mouth in shock. 'I'm sorry, sorry.'

David headed on in and seemed to know where he was going. It must be a local thing, Max thought.

'Why do I get the feeling I'm not going to like this conversation, so?' she said, following. They ended up in a neat little conservatory at the back of the house that Aoife had made into her office. On one side there was a modest desk, opposite was a sofa where David parked himself.

Max didn't know what to do with himself so just blurted out the contents of his brain. 'It's about Carla, Aoife. *And* it's about Lucky.'

Aoife's face didn't break into a look of surprise. She must have known this was coming – well, half of it at least.

David took over and brought Aoife up to speed with current events.

Her poker face broke at the mention of Lucky taking Max's fingers without him asking for a wish, and when he told Aoife about Carla's last wish, and ultimately the fact that Lucky had murdered her, she began crying.

To Max's surprise, David went over to comfort her. He hadn't seen this side of him yet and he wondered how he had loved his sister. Was it in *that* way or in this friendly local way where everyone let themselves into each other's houses and knew where the tea was kept?

'Poor Carla. We all knew the illness had crept up on her but we'd just thought... oh, I don't know... These things happen. Doctor's miss things and then that's it, isn't it? I should have known,' she said.

'Carla would never have agreed to that trade, she wasn't stupid. Lucky did her tricking alright,' David said.

'You're right, she wasn't stupid. She was brilliant. And Lucky is even more so. She's deadly. And not in the good way those young Dubliners say.'

It was hard for Max to hear these kind words spoken about Carla. The gravity of what Max had lost yet again increased.

'What are you two up to?' she continued. 'What are you planning? You're thick to try anything I tell you.'

'We want to kill her. For Carla,' Max said.

Aoife looked at Max but didn't seem to really see him.

'Aoife, maybe it's time we brought an end to all this,' David said.

Max looked at him in shock. Was he on board?

Aoife took a breath that looked to be filled with razor blades and tried to speak, but no words came.

David continued. 'Nobody here really benefits from Lucky. She benefits from us. We're her flock; we feed her. She's been driving us out of town for god knows how long because we know it's not safe to raise kids here. I shudder to think if our ancestors had to learn the hard way. Max may sound crazy, but I think he might be the only one around here with his head screwed on, you know. What Lucky did to Carla is unspeakable. We can't let her get away with this. Even taking Max's fingers like that was wrong. He didn't even ask for a wish. She's never done that before.'

'Look. I know you want to think that Lucky tricked Carla, but that's not how it works,' Aoife said. 'As soon as you step into those woods, all bets are off. We are not the ones in control. You said it David, we're her flock. You may go in willingly, but really she's dragged you down there because she knows human greed will lead us to her door. When Carla asked for Max's forgiveness, Lucky charged her accordingly to get it done. Yes, it was a disgusting thing to do, but we don't set the rules and she doesn't have a rate card. She'll take whatever she wants at the time. A finger, your eyesight or your life. We're all sick in a way and that's what Lucky preys on.'

'But she's never killed, Aoife. This is different and you know it,' David said.

Aoife sat quietly, churning over something that to Max seemed thick as tar and smelled like shit. Finally, she spoke. 'She has done it, David. At least once before. Because I asked her to.'

## 28

After looking around to check there were no soap opera cameras, Max interrupted the silence that had followed Aoife's words. David hadn't said anything but his body seemed to soften in some form of understanding and Max got the impression Aoife hadn't asked for Lucky to go on a killing spree.

'Sorry. Am I missing something?' Max asked.

Aoife gave him a warm smile. 'You are a dote, Maxy. A woman tells you she's had someone killed and you don't run for the hills?'

'You don't strike me as someone who would do something maliciously. You saved Enid. I know that now.' He smiled back and then realised he actually hadn't said thank you for that yet. He spurted it out and she smiled once again.

'Ah well, I don't think it's right for anyone to die unless it's their time. But maybe it was his time after all.' She looked up to David from behind her desk. 'I hope you won't think ill of me David.'

'Cillian?' David asked.

Aoife sighed but didn't acknowledge this with words, only tears.

Max looked around the room and there didn't seem to be any photos that might indicate Aoife had a spouse or a child. Max hoped they weren't speaking about the latter and proceeded respectfully.

'Who was he?'

'My husband. Cillian was my husband and I had him killed.'

'Aoife, you don't need to explain,' David said.

'No. It'll help you understand Lucky better and her malign ways. I know no one talks about her, the biggest worst kept secret that she is, and god knows it might do me some good to talk about it. I never have you see, properly. I tried once at confession but... I feel even God doesn't know all the mysteries of the supernatural and the ways they work. I don't know if he would have understood.'

'We will,' Max said, hoping he didn't sound too manipulative just to get the information he needed.

'You are a dote,' Aoife said once again, and then told her story.

---

'My family have always been the solicitors in Coillte Ádh. Donkey's years they've been at it. They did all the paperwork. Even while my parents were in charge, raising me away in Rinavore, the community came to visit when they needed to, so we got more foot traffic than most. Cillian was a little older than me and we played together whenever his family came. You see Max, they like kids to play with those from the community when they're growing up, it just makes things easier. It doesn't send outsiders running to their parents as we're slowly brainwashed and spill the beans like all kids do.

That's not to say it was an arranged marriage. Carla's wife is evidence that we have free will to choose who we please, but it all seemed to slot into place. I'd had a few *interested parties* while studying law, but you must understand this was a time when courting a lady had its rules. More rules than most men cared to follow, mind you, and there was always the question of their understanding of this place. I always thought it would be nice to come back and take over the family business one day, so that was always in the back of my mind. But who would be happy here with me? A local of course. Maybe what I really did was take the path of least resistance.

Cillian and I were married not long after I returned to Coillte Ádh. We'd both done our growing up. Ah, Jesus. He swooped in with his flowers, his supportive arm, and a smile I adored, I finally knew what it was to be charmed. To be loved. My parents were over the moon of course, and me in my infinite wisdom, fresh from the world of university, and not *wholly* understanding what our little community did just yet, I dived in. I thought I was an adult and I made my own choices, but sometimes I think Lucky was already counting her chickens.'

Max could feel the steady release of tension from Aoife as she spoke. Each memory opened an old wound, each word scorching her lips as they left a dusty box long since forgotten.

'As most people do around here, we went for a wish.

We didn't need it, we were tremendously happy. We had each other and life was grand. I was working at the family practice and Cillian had got a job at the Galway Daily. Neither of us really knew what we wanted. If your family has been here a while, you don't really need money, one of your ancestors would have done that, as long as no one had squandered it away. Well, fifty-fifty on that, truth be told. So, there we were talking to a badger, thinking it was amazing to be so close to one, and off Cillian's tongue rolls. "I want to be the best writer in Ireland!" She giggled at the memory with the heart of the young lady she had been.

'And you?' Max asked.

'Me. Well, I'd always wanted to travel so I asked to speak all the languages of the world. That's why I found it so funny that Cillian had only asked to be the best writer in *Ireland,* the fool. I asked later why he didn't ask "in the world" and he said that James Joyce was on his mind. He was a funny man. Before.'

'And the cost?'

'Ah yes, the cost. We must not forget that, as that's the way things work isn't it? Lucky took his hands.'

'I—' Max started, while his brain brought to vision a badger tearing them both off in a bloody mess.

'Arthritis,' she explained. The horror in which Lucky's mind worked struck Max again. It was mischievous and cruel but also clever.

'I always thought he was a good writer,' David added.

'He was, even before Lucky. But he wanted more. He was churning out stories for the paper at an alarming rate, could have been editor for a national, easy. But he got into his poetry and novels. He became obsessed, burning a hole in the pages when he wrote. It was a little disconcerting to watch, truth be told. He was on the verge of fame when the first signs showed. She's smart. She lets you taste just enough of the good life before she takes. By then, people don't make the connection. They fool themselves. They don't blame her. It's madness. Take Cillian, he thought it was because he was writing too much, his hands whirling away across the page and pounding heavy typewriters. He tried to work through it, drink through it, then eventually went to the doctors and they diagnosed rheumatoid arthritis. I guess they didn't question it too much with his line of work. And neither did he.'

'Ah, Aoife. I'm sorry. I didn't know,' David said.

'And why would you? You know wishers keep to themselves. Although it's kind of you to think my Cillian was *that* naturally talented,' she laughed.

'I know but, his behaviour was—'

'Yes, it was. More drink on top of tablets that might as well have been placebos. He got aggressive. He started directing it at me until the arthritis took that away from him too. He grew ignorant to the fact that he had brought this upon himself. The days I spent arguing with him, refusing to take his feeble body to the woods so he could ask Lucky to fix it, to take it back. But I knew that would cost him a lot more. He even tried to take his own life, but again, he couldn't even get that right. Her cruelty is, well it's cleverly planned. She covers all the exits.

So, there was this man, the most talented writer in all of *Ireland,* but he couldn't write. I understood his frustration. I tried to write for him. I said I could quit my job, be his scribe. But it was like the power flowed through his hands, not just his mind. So, against my better judgement, knowing that Lucky was not to be trusted, I did it. I wished to fix him. I wanted my husband back.'

'Your second wish?' Max asked, a little stunned at how readily people really did seem to use Lucky.

'Well, it's not uncommon to have more than one wish if you haven't been burnt too badly by Lucky, but I never got my first wish. I don't think I'd still have my tongue if I did. Do you?'

'Lucky couldn't grant your first wish?'

'Oh, I know she could have. But that's not the reason. When I asked to speak all the languages under the sun she started to get cryptic about what was under the sun. She rambled on and on, then David tugged at me to leave. So we did. Left her there nattering. Like I said, we were grand and I didn't desire anything that I didn't already have, which is why I guess I never pushed her on it. When were we likely to travel anyway? I've never left Ireland. No, she knew I would be back one day and didn't want to burn me just yet. She had covered her exits. So, when I eventually went down alone for my first and only wish, she saw me coming. I wanted him to be better, to sort his hands out, his body, take away his gift if it meant getting things back to the way they were. But all I managed to cry at her was *"make it stop!"* By the time the words left my mouth, I knew what I'd done.'

'Oh Aoife, I'm so sorry,' Max said.

'He was dead by the time I got home. I didn't even get to say goodbye. And the cost? My sacrifice to her?'

'Your guilt,' Max said, tears in his own eyes now. The same guilt he felt.

'That's the one, Maxy. That's the one. And I live with

125

it every day. That's enough for Lucky. The cunt.'

Max was more terrified of Lucky now than he first thought.

## 29

'So, now you know how horrible she is. Why you shouldn't mess with her. No one ever truly wins,' Aoife said, as composed now as she had been at the start of her recollection.

'No, they don't,' David added in agreement.

'But, if she's so bad, why don't people wise up to Lucky?' Max asked.

'Ah, because we're all feckin' eejits,' David said.

'We're sick Max, all of us. We can't help it. Look at me! I thought I was smart enough to avoid her malicious behaviour and... Well, you know the story now,' Aoife said.

'David. You said you've never made a wish. Is that really true?' Max asked, trying to understand Lucky's grip on people.

'It is. I didn't lie to you.'

'He's a good egg our David. Grumpy fecker that he is,' Aoife gave David a warm smile which he returned.

'So, does that mean you're kind of immune or

something? I mean look at me. I was only around a few days and somehow I managed to succumb to her ways even though I didn't know it. Yes, I went down of my own accord, wanting to see Carla's drawings in the flesh, but what if it was Lucky's lure all along? Subconsciously, I may have known.'

'I don't think I'm immune. Honestly, I think I know what it is: I think I'm too stupid. Too stupid and a lot scared.'

'David you're not stupid. You—' Max started, wholly believing that, ok, he wasn't book smart, but he was street smart, or woods smart, but David cut him off.

'I honestly thought about leaving you be that night Max. Ah, Jesus. I'm sorry to say it, but I did. After you left the pub, I fooled myself thinking you'd just gone on home.' David's face dropped into hopelessness. 'I kept telling myself to leave you be, that it wasn't my business. Just like everyone else around here, *leave them be*. I can't change their minds and I doubt anyone would listen even if I tried. But something made me follow you. I think it was Carla, talking to me somehow, from deep inside. I lied to you. I've had those rock salt shells for years but I've never done anything with them. I was just plain avoiding you. I was scared to use them and still surprised that I did. I went into some kind of autopilot when I caught sight of you entering the woods from the top of the hill. Ah Max, I'm sorry for the lies. I'm just an old stupid tool. That's why Lucky doesn't bother with me, and although I hate myself for saying it, I don't think we should bother with her. I'm sorry for riling you up, riling *me* up again. I thought together we might do it, but she's too smart for us.'

Max's stomach followed the tracks of a very shaky

rollercoaster as David laid it all bare, and yet again felt very alone in this little village. Not that he wholly blamed David for that, it was this place. Max had been thrust into a world that was not his own and he wished for just a moment, just a flicker of a thought, that he'd never picked up the phone and had never opened up this door to his past again. But that was a dark alley to go down. Ultimately, the real reason any of this had happened was because he had been a bad brother.

'Lads, I'm sorry,' Aoife said. 'I truly am. But this isn't a fight you can win. Look at us three, we're no musketeers and we've each been burnt in our own way.'

Aoife looked longingly to David for approval and eventually he nodded.

*Damn that nod.*

She then turned her eyes to Max and already feeling the fight drain from his body, he avoided her gaze. He focused on the spot between his feet and realised they were trembling. His body was already telling him to run. He felt tears brew again and soon enough his vision blurred and the first drop hit the floor. It was done. He looked up to Aoife, she was smiling that kind smile. He hadn't realised it before but she was quite beautiful. Behind the assertive manner, behind the stoic solicitor and her bright wellies, she was beautiful and trustworthy. Max couldn't speak, so he took a leaf from David's book, nodded, and let himself out.

---

## 30

Max didn't play any more records as he cleaned up the following day. In fact, he moved the entire box across from the neat "keep" stack to the mess that was the "bin" pile. There were too many memories between those sleeves and now they had been tarnished with terror. Max wasn't one for wasting, especially when it came to good vinyl, but if he donated them as they were, someone might find Carla's drawings, and he feared they might hold the power to pull strangers into the woods. That meant he would have to go through each one checking she hadn't left anymore and each time he found one, and he knew he *would* find one, he would be reminded of his failure to avenge her death, and his failure as a brother in the years that preceded it. He decided to let Nirvana, The Beatles, Tom Petty and the gang rot away their covers and sleeves in a stinking landfill until shards of vinyl broke through and sang their final tune to a passing magpie.

As the day went on, Max found himself moving more and more out of the keep stack and into the donate pile until all that remained was a single piece of jewellery. A delicate gold necklace with a small circular pendant pressed with a Celtic harp. He slid the chain between his hands feeling the satisfying slink and coil of the chain, and then tossed it across the empty room. It could stay here. The best thing was to go back to the way life had been before coming to Coillte Ádh, pretending he didn't have a sister at all, something he used to be very good at. He was sure that over time he'd forget this incident and it would all feel like a very bad dream. He looked down to his left hand but unfortunately the fingers were still gone. That would serve as a reminder. He still had to explain that one to Nat.

After making a pitiful lunch with the out-of-date supplies he'd bought over a week ago, and a few tinned items Carla had in her cupboards, Aoife stopped by. She was back to her normal self, walking by Max at the door and slapping down the final pieces of paperwork that needed signing. She said she'd take care of the piles of belongings and the sale of the house. She hoped to have a local family in, who were due back from their "time away" by the end of the year. She asked what Max might do with the money and he absently said she could burn it. Sensing he was finally in real mourning, she touched his shoulder gently, and for a second he saw the ghosts of last night in her eyes. They left as soon as she let go. Max did a final sweep of the house to ensure he'd done all he needed to do, then put the kettle on one last time and sank into that armchair for a final goodbye. He could feel the mountain of Carla's items staring at him, judging him. "Aren't we good enough for you either, Maxy? No time for your sister and no time for her things?"

'Ah, fuck off,' he said to them. They said nothing in reply. Max went to pour out the boiled water, but he didn't return to the armchair. Instead, he took his tea through to Carla's room. He'd spent as little time as possible in there and whenever he did, he avoided the nagging stare of the bed. "Didn't come to visit your sister on her deathbed, tut tut."

*Does everything in this house have to taunt me?*

He went round the barren room and tried to imagine the final hours of her life. Was she alone? Was David by her side? Was the village at the door? Max took a sip of his tea and thought about David and Carla's relationship. It wasn't odd for people to fall in love again when a spouse had died, especially in a small place like this. Perhaps it was just companionship. Either way, Max was happy for that. Old wounds, he thought looking down at his hand. The bandages were an unblemished white, finally. The seeping of blood and whatever else the body did in these situations had now stopped. Once again, he was unable to get a handle on his thoughts.

*Money, fame, fortune, sex, money, sex, lots of sex, sex with lots of different people, all at once.*

His crotch started to vibrate and then the tinny crackle of a ringtone came from his pocket. He came back to the room and immediately realised he was panting. He had to get out of this place. He pulled out his phone and saw it was Nat.

*Thank fuck for Nat.*

'Hey darling,' he said, eager to hear her voice and hoping the reception would hold.

'Max? Ah good, I wasn't sure if I'd get through.' Nat sounded rather chirpy.

'Yup, yup. I can hear you.'

'How you feeling? You sound out of breath.'

'Oh? Just eager to get home and see you both. I miss you.'

'Oh Max. I miss you too. We miss you.'

'How's Enid been?' No reply. 'Nat?'

'Max?'

'Bloody line. How's Enid?' he said, louder, as if that would fix the reception.

'Oh, you're back. Yeah, she's a little grumpy. She misses her daddy.'

'Good. She's not forgotten me then?'

'Not quite,' she said. 'Where are you now?'

'Just at Carla's, finishing up. I'll be leaving in an hour or so. I booked a hotel near the airport.'

'No, don't do that.' Nat said.

'What?' Silence again. 'Nat? Are you there?'

'Yup. I just thought you'd stay there another night.'

'Yeah, I have to return the car, then there's traffic and early flights and all that.'

'Ok. Well, make sure you've got everything. Double check. Leaving in an hour, did you say? If you're worried about traffic, there's no point leaving now, anyway. It's kick out time for work.'

'Oh, yeah, that's a good point. Maybe I'll pop and see David.'

'The neighbour?'

'Yeah. We've ended up getting quite…' *so many words,* 'close.'

'Well that sounds nice. Ok bubba. I gotta run. Can't wait to see you.'

'You and me both. I love you.'

'I love you too,' Nat said, then hung up.

Max put the phone down on the counter and looked round the room one last time but he didn't really take it in. Something was up. What was it? He looked at the phone as if hoping it might reveal the answer to this suddenly burning question, but it lay there silently with its screen off.

What *was* it? His heart took an uncomfortable beat, then suddenly decided to up its pace without warning. He picked up the phone and went to dial Nat, his thumb hovering above the screen.

*What was it?*

He hit call and raised the phone to his ear. One ring, two rings, the penny dropped on the third ring.

*No.*

That was a local dial tone. Nat was in Ireland.

## 31

'David! David!' Max shouted, hammering on his door, 'David it's Max. Enid is coming, she's coming here now!' Falling over his feet, Max stumbled backwards out of David's drive then turned and ran back inside to get the car keys. 'Fuck, fuck, fuck.'

His eyes came to rest on the fireplace tools and he burned with fright. He had nothing, no weapons. He needed David.

*The salt!*

He tried to dial through to Nat again but she didn't answer. She was either being coy about her surprise visit and that he had pieced it together or–

*Don't you go thinking that. She's not in those woods yet.*

He ran into the bedroom and picked up the salt tin. It was very light from the decanting the other night. A moan escaped his mouth.

'Max?' It was David.

'David! Thank fuck,' Max said, running back outside. David's hair was all ruffled and he had a look of terror on his face greater than anything Max had seen yet. He had his shotgun broken over his arm but it looked limp, like it wasn't up to the task, like it didn't *want* to do the task, because it knew it was futile. But they had to try.

'David. Enid! Nat's come back to Ireland to surprise... She's—' he said.

'I heard, I heard. Keep it down. Where are they?'

'I don't know, she's not answering. Come on, we have to go. If Lucky...' Max started, but didn't want to tempt fate anymore as he ran to the car. It roared into life at the snap of the key; he had his steed.

David took a worried glance around, then made his choice. He got in the car quickly and Max shot it out the drive and down the road. As they approached Aoife's, David shouted to stop then leant across and blasted the horn on the steering wheel three times.

'Wait,' David said.

Aoife's house was silent.

'David! I can't,' Max said, planting his foot again and sending the Skoda zipping off down the hill. He blasted the horn as he went, hoping Aoife would hear the distress signal.

Everything looked normal as they entered Lucky's Woods. As always, the sun was shining overhead and it looked like an inviting place for a picnic. More importantly, there were no taxis or rental cars in sight. Max let off the accelerator for a more thorough look but was relieved to see nothing more, not even a deer.

'Nothing here,' David also confirmed, shuffling the

shotgun awkwardly in his seat. He wouldn't be able to do much with that long barrel in the car. The road ahead was clear but Max was eager to get round the bend and check the final stretch, then they could just block the road and wait it out. He kicked the accelerator to the floor and the car dropped down a gear. They shot off once again. Max's heart thumped as the car hugged a corner which seemed to go on forever. When he made it past the apex, the road opened up to reveal the exit to the woods and the most bizarre and terrifying scene Max had ever seen.

*When will this nightmare end?*

Ahead of them on the road was a sea of dead, battered and twitching woodland creatures. There were different types of deer, badgers, foxes, squirrels and countless birds forming a splatter pattern emanating from a mangled car. There was a large *TAXI* sticker on the driver door. The windscreen was completely caved in, and the body of not one but two deer were protruding out, the legs rigid as if they were still in flight. The radiator grill had been shattered and a fox was hanging out of it, its hind legs just touching the road as if it were sniffing inside the engine bay for titbits. Birds peppered the rest of the vehicle like Lucky had tried her hand at a Pollock painting.

Max was so lost in the devastation he nearly ran over some of the animals that had been flung outwards from the impact. He brought the car to an abrupt stop and got out, he went to shout for Nat and Enid but the air was thick with death. What had Lucky done? She'd gone completely overboard, from the one deer she placed last week to seemingly everything that lived in the forest. She was desperate, but it had done the job. He heard the metallic click of David's shotgun but couldn't pull his eyes away from the carnage, then Max heard the sound of a baby crying, which broke the trance and he dashed towards the wreck.

'Enid!'

His view was blocked through the taxi's windscreen. As he approached the driver's door he felt slick saliva fill his mouth at the sight of the driver, or what was left of her. Once again, Max struggled to avert his gaze from this fresh horror. Her head had been completely crushed against the restraint by the force of the deer entering. He wasn't even sure she'd had a chance to reach the airbag first.

His legs shakily took his upper body another couple of steps to the rear of the car and there he saw Nat, his beautiful Nat. In a flash, he took in the large gash on her forehead and also the quick, laboured, rise and fall of her chest. She was alive. His eyes skidded across to the other side and the empty child seat. Another groan escaped from behind his teeth, and an absolutely gut wrenching pain pulled down on everything inside, threatening to evacuate his organs onto the road. His head went for a swim but he clawed it back to shore.

'Nat, Nat,' he said, gently placing a hand on her shoulder. On closer inspection, there was nothing impaling her, but he wasn't too sure of her condition. 'Nat. It's Max.'

She slowly licked her lips and went to speak but only managed a whisper. 'Enid.'

David reached his side. 'Ah Christ, no. We need to call an ambulance.'

Max turned to David for help but didn't know what

either of them could do, he had to find Enid. 'Enid!' he shouted again. He went to take the phone out of his pocket knowing there was likely to be as much signal here as there was in the Mariana Trench. Then he heard a cry again, more distant.

David's hand now found Max's shoulder. He held out the gun. 'Go!' he said.

'David, I've never shot one. You need to do it.'

'Ah, stop. I'll never catch up with her, I'm too old.' He started to dig into his own pocket. 'Take these spare cartridges. That's all I've got.' He placed two red rock salt shells in his hand.

'But I don't…'

'Max stop fucking around you dryshite!' David said with a force Max hadn't before witnessed. All sympathy had gone from his features, and all that remained was anger. 'You aim, you shoot, you snap the barrel, you reload.' He pointed to a switch near the trigger. 'You've seen a fucking film, now go,' and he thrust the shotgun into Max with such force that he stumbled against the car.

The weight of the gun seemed to stir something inside him. It was like the night he held the poker, but he *knew* this weapon worked. Now he fished in his own pockets but instead of cartridges, he pulled out his phone, unlocked it and gave it to David.

'Code is 1111.'

'1111,' David repeated.

He took one last survey of Nat. He felt mildly reassured that she was only concussed. Max ran around the car, skipped over more carcasses and broke into the forest. He turned back one last time, but he wished he hadn't. The scene that lay before him was all too familiar. It was the exact spot where Lucky had stood in his vision. It was a premonition. Somehow, she knew Nat would be back with Enid. Max made off into the forest but didn't look down to see if the forest floor was alive – that would surely strip the last little bit of confidence he had away.

## 32

With no path to guide him this time, Max staggered aimlessly among the bushes but tried to keep going away from the road as much as possible. His mind was running amuck. Half was yelling at him to return to Nat, the other half pushing him on towards his daughter. Then there was another part, somehow squeezing itself between the two halves and creating a new medium. Fear and doubt. It repeated the same word over and over.

*Run. Run. Run.*

Max flung the words aside and ploughed on. He could still hear Enid's pained cries but they weren't constant, and with the rustling underfoot it was hard to run and listen at the same time. He felt like he was in an agonising Olympic race. False start after false start he was getting closer to the finish line, only for it to advance again each time he stopped to listen. It was killing him not being able to close the distance faster. He held the shotgun close to his body, gripping it with his remaining fingers as he ran, and tried to familiarise himself with the controls as he went. David was right, he knew the general idea, and after the third time stopping to listen he tried the lever to break the gun and was greeted with the brass back end of two cartridges. That made him feel better. He just hoped he'd be able to hit something – he only had the two spares in his pocket.

The forest was eerily still. There were no birds chirping when he stopped to listen for Enid's breadcrumb trail of cries. No hooves crunching fallen leaves, no squirrels bounding through the trees, and not even the buzz of insects. Lucky had thrown absolutely everything at that taxi to bring it to a stop. He was sure even the earthworms had been conscripted, had he the time and inclination to start digging and check.

Enid's crying became more and more constant until its sustained pitch matched the previous times they'd driven through the woods. Perhaps Enid had also been concussed from the accident. If Lucky hurt Enid—

*You'll what, shit your pants again? Run.*

The constant cry allowed him to get closer and soon it was louder than the crunching underfoot – he was getting close. He went to shout out Enid's name but caught his tongue before the words escaped. What would be the use of announcing himself? Max decided to keep quiet, even if Lucky did know he was following. Soon after, he was rewarded with the brief sight of a shimmering beetle-like back through the dense forest. Lucky had come out.

His body froze and it wasn't until Lucky had disappeared behind some thick trunks that he followed on, this time with the shotgun raised. Might he get retribution for his daughter *and* his sister now? How far would the shot go? Would Enid be ok? He wasn't a ballistics expert but he doubted rock salt went as far as normal buckshot did. Then there was all the thick forest between them.

He stroked the arm that David had peppered and barely winced. At least he felt more comfortable knowing that should anything hit Enid, it was unlikely to be fatal – to her. Lucky however, would burn. He pressed on, and each time Lucky came into view, Max's heart thumped wildly. What *was* she? That shimmering back was mesmerising.

*You can't kill her. Run.*

Yes, he could. He couldn't make out Enid but he could tell from the positioning of Lucky's elbows that she was cradling her. He found this odd at first but what did he expect? Lucky to be dragging his child along the ground by a leg? Max slowly closed the distance between them but still had no clear shot. After losing Lucky again behind some Oak saplings, Enid's cries were cut off abruptly. He stopped walking thinking the worst. Blood ran from his face and he felt cold all over. She wouldn't come all this way then suddenly take Enid's life.

*Wouldn't she? Run Maxy. RUN!*

'Oh shut up!' he screamed at himself, then quickly slapped a hand over his mouth like a mime that had broken the unwritten rule. His new passenger didn't taunt him for his outburst; he knew he'd messed up.

'Enid!' he cried, giving away his advantage – if he did ever have any. Max ran forward with the shotgun raised and packed against his shoulder like he'd seen in the films, going around the young oaks in the opposite direction Lucky had done. His heart was beating violently and he thought that even if he had kept his mouth shut the sound would have betrayed him. He glanced down to the shotgun one last time checking that what he believed to be the safety was off, and placed his finger delicately on the trigger. He reached the edge where the trees opened, jumped through, tripped, and without meaning to, fired a low shot which shook his body and snapped his eyes shut. He had to be more delicate with the trigger.

## 33

Max tried to recover his composure and flung the shotgun left and right looking for a target but saw nothing. He looked down for a scratched Enid and Lucky's burning carcass but saw nothing but fallen leaves and mud. No body and *no* Enid. He kept spinning wildly around in search of them. Nothing. He stood quietly listening but still nothing. Panic started to take over. Had he lost her forever? Where had they gone? Max fumbled at the shotgun and pain shot through his stubs as they knocked against the barrel. He managed to break it, found the spent one and replaced it with another from his pocket. That left one lonely cartridge in his jeans pocket like the limp attempt of a man trying to pad out his endowment. He snapped the shotgun back together and paced round once more in search of them both, his hope draining with each step, each footprint a mark of his failure.

'Lucky!' Perhaps he could draw her out. 'Lucky, show yourself.'

Nothing.

'Enid!'

Nothing.

He pressed on in the direction Lucky had been going and soon passed a tremendously large tree with clumps of small red berries. He stopped dead. He examined the leaves – small and lobbed. It was a hawthorn, but it was gigantic. He walked backwards taking in the size of the tree. It must have easily been over twenty metres. And the trunk, it was gargantuan. He'd never seen anything like it. Was it beautiful, or was it wrong? Carla's depiction had been of a hawthorn in bloom, but it wasn't hard to tell this was the same tree looking down at the exposed roots, and what at first he thought comically sized on paper seemed threateningly less so in the flesh. He ran around the tree both hoping and not hoping he would find the opening – the most disturbing part of Carla's sketch. For if he found the opening, he would have to enter.

There it was.

His mouth dried in an instant and he was sure his tongue had shrivelled to a raisin. Should he run back and get David, Nat, the police, the army? Would he even be able to find his way back to them? Would he then be able to get back to the tree? He'd been following Enid's cries but not paying attention to where he'd been going; it was all a blur. There was no time. He moved towards the hole and wondered why he was being so contemplative about this. Lucky had his daughter, his only daughter that he loved with all his heart. But the madness of the situation still caused a disconnect between the reality of the situation and the consequences. It was as if the fear for her hadn't been strong enough, but now she was gone. The reality set in, and it was visceral. *Come on, you got this.* Finally, he seemed to believe in himself.

Max approached the hole, still continuing to check over his shoulder in case of ambush. He was wired now, acutely focused. The grey depicted in Carla's drawings took on a deep darkness in real life, but he steadied his breathing and it became less intimidating with each exhale. He thought he might have to get down and crawl through the burrow, but as he got nearer it seemed to expand, or was he shrinking? He had to crouch a little but still managed to fit inside easily. The darkness was instant the moment his peripherals were covered. He got the feeling if he looked over his shoulder he would see nothing but darkness all around. He was submerged.

Max wasn't sure how long he went on but he ignored the burning that was building in his crouched legs. With his eyes useless, his ears picked up the nuances of the path. Openings came occasionally to the left and right. He wasn't sure what kind of labyrinth this was, but something told him to head straight and he trusted it. Something his subconscious had been privately chewing over was that reality as he knew it was no more. Lucky had shown him that. If she could grant wishes and curse locals, what's to say Max couldn't do something more than human? He could sense his daughter.

Soon, Max felt his weight shift into the front of his knees. He thought he was going deeper underground, but then a peculiar feeling came over him. The weight kept shifting up his knees until his brain told him he was on a very steep decline, but his footing was telling him something else. There was no slipping and sliding, his feet were getting heavy, as if he were wearing an enormous pair of boots. Boots that seemed to cling to the earth like a magnet would to iron. His stomach started to mimic the motion as if he was about to go head over heels. With nowhere else to go he proceeded on with incremental steps, each one taking more effort as the weight in his feet increased, until he felt all the blood rush to his head - there was no doubt he was now upside down - but he was still crouching to avoid banging his head on the earthy ceiling. His mind and body were frantically arguing at the physics of the situation and he grinded his teeth in frustration. Time was slipping away while he navigated this bizarre maze and he cursed Lucky for it. Enid needed him, he couldn't fuck around in this place any longer. The steps were almost unbearable now, his feet almost glued to the earth. With a scream Max managed another step and then the entire world flipped under him. He gasped as he threw his free hand out to catch himself. His feet thudded the floor as if they hadn't seen firm ground in a long time and the entire tunnel vibrated around him, shaking loose earth free which showered him from all around. He felt upright once more. Without missing a beat he headed on. At last, Max saw the light at the end of the tunnel. He cast aside the scent of magical wonder from the events behind him and headed off towards the twilight with a confident stride, not bumping his head once.

## 34

Max heard the crying as soon as he stepped out. What sweet relief. His eyes adjusted to the purple twilight he now stood in, and he saw he was in another forest, but everything was wrong. He spun around and his eyes rolled up the tree but didn't quite make it to the sky. There was no hawthorn in its midsummer best, its leaves green and berries bursting. There were only roots. Roots that were softly swaying in the air like the tentacles of a bathing jellyfish. Max looked around the forest. It was all wrong, there were only trees made of swaying roots. It was as if the ground had been flipped and all the soil shaken away. What fresh hell was this? Max's brain gawped at the unnatural way they were swaying. They weren't swaying in a summer breeze, they were *alive,* reaching out into the nether for... for what? Sustenance? What if he became their sustenance, their compost to feed on? His ears started ringing, drowning out Enid's cries. He imagined the long roots reaching down and whipping him up, stretching him out limb by limp like a sail in the wind then thrusting a long sharp root deep into his throat to eat him from the inside out.

*Stop it!*

His consciousness finally came to the rescue.

*You have to get to Enid.*

Yes.

*Breath.*

Max took a very deep breath, got the popping tinkle of a full set of lungs then slowly exhaled to get his bearings. The crying found his ears once again and Max followed the sound. The upended hawthorn seemed to be the tallest "tree" but there were small delicate roots at ankle height, spindly finger-like ones from knee to head, and then larger muscular ones dotted around. His fear dissipated. If the trees wanted him, they would have had him by now.

He quickly honed in on Enid's crying and was once again in pursuit. Whether or not Lucky had heard the shotgun blast, or his shouts through the tunnel, remained to be seen. He kept a low profile once again. Without any foliage Enid's cries were carrying easily through the silent root forest but Max found it hard to gauge how close he was. The effect was disorienting but within a few minutes, the roots thinned out and he was gobsmacked to find a dirt road that very much looked like the one above – or was it below now?

Whatever it was, Max was confident he was in a complete replica of the world above, but from an *inside* perspective. At least he knew his way around, a little. He skirted the edge of the forest with the road at his side not wanting to break cover completely. He looked out towards Coillte Ádh but it wasn't there. There was no rocky hill cut against this deep cosmic purple sky, just a flat black horizon. Could it really be down in a valley? Well, if the forest was anything to go by, it could well be. Hills would be valleys, mountains would be canyons. Another burst of crying carried through the air but the light was too low to make anything out. His gut tugged once more and he followed it across the fields of soft spongy soil, leaving the forest and their swaying roots behind him. The sky was dotted with vivid stars but there didn't seem to be any dominant light source – no moons, no suns. Just perpetual twilight adding to the calm silence.

It was quick going across the fields but hard to see deep into the valley. He headed down the hill, or more so, he headed *into* the hill. He had to drag his mind back to the task again as he pictured what the Himalayas must look like here. Max looked around and tried to gauge where he was in the town but the starkest difference was the lack of buildings in this version of Coillte Ádh – there was little cover. Like a poorly trained spy he followed Enid's staccato cries and sobs in and out of dark rises in the ground that would be ditches on the other side, ducked behind the occasional root system of a small tree and even a couple of tall cylindrical pillars of stone which he thought might be wells. *Madness.*

While taking shelter behind a tight cluster of swaying roots the unmistakable glow of firelight suddenly filled the silent landscape and cast flickering shadows across this deserted village. Max hit the ground fast and spread out to make himself as flat as possible, he felt the moisture of the ground permeate his clothes and the earthy smell of soil puffed into his nose. The crying was there but it was muffled, Lucky had taken Enid inside something. Peaking through the low swaying roots he easily picked out the source of the glow, it was coming from a large hut which looked to be made of roots. Max shuffled the shotgun around ignoring the pain in his hand, there was nothing between him and the hut, he would have to rise with the shotgun poised and ready to strike. This was it. He held the gun tightly.

He slowly raised from the ground, not stopping to brush off the clinging dirt and moved forward. He'd made it one step when he heard a soft hissing behind him. It sounded just like the striking of a match, then something wet struck him on the back of his head. A cold tingling feeling oozed outwards from his cerebellum and he lost his balance. The ground came up fast to meet his face. Then it all went dark – again.

## 35

'Daddy,' Enid said.

Please darling, I'm trying to sleep, Max thought as he lay on his back trying to get some more winks in. This bed was *hard!*

'Daddy,' she repeated, now thumping Max with her little fists. Ergh, the days of being able to sleep in, how you are missed, how little you were valued.

More thumping.

Max went to say he was getting up, but he didn't quite articulate the words well enough. He felt around in his mouth with his tongue; it all seemed to be working but there was an odd taste – off, damp, earthy. Then it all came back to him.

Adrenaline filled his body and he felt a weight on his chest. He opened his eyes. Enid was there, inches from his face. Beautiful Enid, she was safe. He had her, they were safe. But how?

'Daddy up!' she cheered happily, slapping his face with her little hands.

'Enid,' he now managed clearly, 'where's mummy?'

Enid looked sad at this and tears began to well in her eyes. Her shoulders convulsed in bursts, then out came the cries followed by that infinite stream of sticky snot from her nose.

'Some wet nurse you are,' said a female voice. It wasn't Nat.

His fear returned; they weren't safe. It was Lucky. He jolted to get up. He managed his head but everything else stayed glued to the ground. When did Enid get so heavy? He frantically tried to roll over. His head went but again his body stayed planted. He tried to twitch a finger, nothing. He was paralyzed from the neck down. Something stirred nearby. He saw Enid's eyes grow wide with fear and uncertainty, she let out one more cry.

'Silence!' Lucky said.

Enid snapped her mouth shut and buried herself into Max's chest. The snatcher had returned. 'That crying is insufferable. She thinks I'm an evil auntie now you are present. She listens.'

With Enid in his chest, Max now had a clear view of the ceiling while the fire crackled loudly away. It was woven from tree roots, shaped expertly to form the roof of the hut – the hut from outside that he was now no doubt *inside*. Then, from the top of his vision came a face, Lucky's face. He finally laid eyes on it. She looked human for the most part, but what struck him was that her face was ageless. It was covered in neither the soft plump skin of a baby nor the ravaged leather of an ancient hag. It hung suspended in space as if time didn't know what to do with it. Her wild hair fell down around her face in loose curls. Rather than grace him with her naked form, as she had done until now, she had spared him the embarrassment and was wrapped in interlacing robes of thin moss-like fabric. Her hands fell into view and Max saw that iridescent gloss twinkling on the backs of her hands and running up her arms.

'Welcome,' she said.

Max stared back blankly, at a loss.

'Not what you expected?'

He managed a slight groan but that was all.

'I know you can speak. The spell wears off from the top down. It's why you woke up.' Lucky's eyes shifted to Enid. 'That and that noisy spawn of yours.' She left his vision once again. Her footsteps were soft, delicate, almost imperceptible.

'What have you done to me?' Max said, trying to sound unphased.

'That's a rather broad question, don't you think?'

'Don't—'

'You are paralyzed,' she answered, no doubt sensing that Max was grumbling inside. 'I couldn't have you running around with that barbaric tool, you might hurt someone. It will be hours before the rest of the spell fades.'

'I don't need that thing to hurt you,' Max said.

Lucky chuckled lightly, it was eerily adolescent in tone. 'You *are* a changed man. Travelling through the burrow, finding your way. I didn't think you had it in you. I didn't think any human did anymore. It's been centuries since anyone dared cross over.' She let out a sigh. 'In fact it's been centuries since *I* crossed over. I suppose you have me to thank for your renewed vigour, and I have you to thank for this gift.' She looked to Enid in a thirsty way.

Enid gripped Max tightly and tried to bury her head even deeper into his paralyzed chest. Max knew Enid was still a while off reciting Shakespeare, but her understanding of language was mostly grasped. She could quickly snap out of situations, be distracted onto the next, but she knew something terrible was happening, and it hurt him badly not knowing if he could save her from it.

'What do you want with her?' he asked.

Lucky returned to his vision so quickly and silently it gave Max's head a jolt.

'It is not I that wants her. It is The Dark One.'

'The Dark One? Well, they're not fucking—' Max started but an acute pain ruptured in his right ear and his head snapped sideways.

A short cry escaped Enid.

Lucky had struck him with the speed of a kickboxer. He hadn't felt the connection, only the effect. A ringing started up a warmth pooled in his ear.

'Blasphemy,' Lucky simply said. She walked off again. The Dark One? Surely there weren't greater evils than Lucky.

*Of course there were.*

'You are to travel with us. Your child is noisy and I fear I might do something regrettable if it persists. Not to mention those we will pass, beast or otherwise. You will keep her quiet. I must prepare.'

Travel? Where on this earth were they going? Max summarised this wasn't important. What was important was this gave him time, or give his saviour David time if he was on his tail yet.

*Nat!*

He hoped they'd been able to stabilise her. While

Lucky prepped, he could figure out a way to kill her – *good luck* – or escape, at the least – *sure*. It looked as if his doubt had returned. If he could just grab Enid and get back to his world, he bet he'd stand a chance there. He just needed to get out of the forest, her jurisdiction. All was not lost.

With Lucky out of view, Max tried to move his body once again. It felt as if his shoulders moved a little, but it was almost negligible. He used the full motion of his eyes and head to take in more surroundings. He appeared to be near the side of the hut. At his feet were the winding roots, and on either side seemed to be some sort of seating which he found odd.

*Do monsters sit?*

Craning his head back, he was able to make out the top of Lucky's head in a side room. She was facing away and busying herself with something that sounded a lot like packing and that's when he saw it, propped up against the side. The tip of the shotgun. Forgetting he was paralyzed he made to go for it. His body did not react, but his shoulders… they released. He gave them a little shrug and there they went, rising and falling. Lucky's spell was wearing off already! At this rate, he'd be free in minutes, forget hours, but he had to be careful.

The shotgun wasn't too far away. It would take a few strides when his legs were free, but Lucky might be done by then, the opportunity gone. He probably had time to drag himself, make it across and let a shot loose before she realised. Or even better, he could try a shot from here; there was no way he would miss. He was sure some of the rock salt would make it, then the embers would take over and do the rest – if the deer was anything to go by. He hoped it was. He looked back to Enid who had since dug herself out of his chest, interested in what her father had been doing.

In his softest voice, he asked, 'Do you want to play a game, Enid?'

## 36

Max checked on Lucky again. She was still busy. He looked back to Enid and continued the training; he was pretty sure Enid got the jist. He wasn't proud of it – no child should be conscripted to play with guns at such a young age. But the other outcome was bleak.

'Enid, where's the gun?' he asked, his voice hidden under the crackling fire. Max really mouthed the word to drill it home.

Enid paused for a moment, standard practice based on these sorts of activity, then suddenly pointed one little finger towards the shotgun.

'Good girl,' he whispered.

She started to move off his chest but he flapped his elbows and wriggled his upper body to stop her.

'No, no. Not now.'

At home, this was a simple find and retrieve game they played, something she was actually very good at. Here, however, with all the false starts, she was getting worked up at the constant change in commands. He had to make sure she had it though. The paralysis had worn down to his forearms and he was sure his fingers would be free to wiggle soon. He could risk crawling there but Enid might think he was playing a game and make too much noise. Occupying her was best.

Enid was oddly content sitting on his chest and kept her nattering to a minimum, clearly still wary of evil auntie Lucky. She looked deep into his eyes with a fervency he'd not thought possible from her. She was either deeply invested in the upcoming task or she truly knew the situation they were in, and was using these last few minutes together to search in her father's soul for some answer to the meaning of life.

She would come up short. If either of them were likely to know that, it would be Enid. She smiled as if she'd read his thoughts and flopped forward to give him a hug as he lay on the ground.

His hands followed without argument: he was free. Now would have been the chance to send Enid before the opportunity was missed and Lucky returned to the room, but he didn't want to let go. It had been too long since he'd had the chance to hold Enid and it only hit him now how much he'd missed her. He squeezed her tighter and she reciprocated. A snooker ball of a lump rolled up his throat and wedged itself tight against his Adam's apple. He was going to burst with emotion but he had to keep it in. It would surely bring Lucky through, and when she saw it was not Enid but him crying, she might decide to get rid of his babysitting skills after all. He pulled Enid back and placed his giant hands on her little pebble shoulders.

'Enid, can you get Daddy the gun please?' he whispered.

She slipped off his chest with a dexterity far beyond what he thought possible and waddled towards the shotgun. He rotated as much as he could to check on Lucky; she was still engrossed in her preparation. Enid arrived at the shotgun, which stood a good foot taller than her, and looked back to Max, she wanted to double check this was what the topic of conversation had been all along.

He nodded back vigorously.

Enid placed her hands on the shotgun and then it struck Max like a wet mackerel: she wouldn't be able to lift it.

*You fucking idiot.*

He panicked and started to wriggle on the floor.

Enid fumbled and fumbled but couldn't get a good grip on the wide adult sized contours of the weapon, she waltzed with it on the spot like a drunken sailor but even pulling it away from the wall seemed to take all her strength. She turned and looked back at Max with the biggest bottom lip he had ever seen. The disappointment was palpable; she wanted to complete the task.

He tried to reassure her from this distance but he couldn't console her.

Her face scrunched, her skin turned a violent shade of magenta, then she pushed it away and it crashed to the ground.

His eyes shot to Lucky. She was still facing away but she wasn't busying herself anymore, her shoulders were up at her ears in frustration. They were made! He heaved onto his front, just like he'd seen Enid do many months before. He cocked his shoulders and shot himself across the floor as fast as he could towards Enid and the shotgun.

Enid burst into tears as he approached, shocked at the scene.

He darted his eyes through the doorway and saw Lucky drop whatever she had been doing and look over her shoulder.

She took in the scene and no doubt remembered what she had left just out of sight. Lucky unnaturally snapped her entire body around on the spot as if she was spring loaded and took a step forward, but it was too late.

Max was at the shotgun and wheeling it around to aim. Now *he* had a magic trick. He took aim towards the doorway, flat on his stomach and pushed Enid aside with the barrel.

She went tumbling but she would be ok.

The shot was clean, there was no way he could miss, not in this enclosed space; it was perfect. No heroic words came to mind, no final monologue of how evil never prevails, just a savage lick of his lips and the taste of retribution that Carla deserved, that Aoife deserved, that his bloody fingers deserved! He pulled the trigger and Lucky let out a piercing scream like a banshee. The force of the blast sent her flying backwards into the little room, her legs gave way and she collapsed to the ground.

'Yaaaaaaaaar!' he roared. His body was tingling with adrenaline. He'd fucking done it. Max panted while Enid continued to cry at the side, but he couldn't pull his eyes away from Lucky to calm his daughter. Something didn't seem quite right. The shotgun hadn't kicked like before, had it even made a noise? Where was the smoke? He aimed it again and pulled the trigger, it clicked but nothing happened. Then he heard that adolescent laugh once more and despair spread over him like a bad rash.

## 37

Max broke the shotgun with shaking hands and was greeted with two empty barrels, they took on a vivid darkness, deeper than the burrow at the base of the tree. Two black holes he wished he and Enid could dive into, regardless of the doom. It would be better than this nightmare, this sick game Lucky was playing with him. Lucky had removed the ammunition, of course she had. It was a trick; one last gag before the end.

Her laugh continued and rose to a cackle.

Max looked back to Lucky.

She was still half-playing dead, her body slumped against the wall but her shoulders were jiggling with each soulless laugh that escaped her. The hysterics ebbed and she gracefully picked herself up off the floor, almost floating like she weighed nothing more than a feather.

'That was very much worth the wait. The paralysis actually took longer to fade than I thought, I was running out of things to pack. You really are weak, *Maxy*.'

'You fucking bitch.'

'Yes, yes, yes, I've heard it all. Sure, I like to play games. But you can be awfully predictable, you humans. It's always the same. You willingly come, make your wishes. Yet it is me that is the problem. You humans never look inwards to find that most everything is *your* fault. You selfish beings. You destroy the land, yet you want crops. You poison the seas, yet you fish. You have no love for your own kind and then cry like children when *you* are mistreated. Who do you really think killed your sister Max? Would she have come to me if you had been a fairer brother?' Max's emotions went spiralling off chaotically and Lucky didn't wait for the answer. 'Of course not. She was a good woman, I saw her heart. A selfless request and I read between the lines. She wasn't asking for *you* to forgive her. She had done nothing wrong. She was asking for you to grow up and stop being so petulant. I'm not even sure it worked. You're clearly still naive if you thought you could better me. You're all pathetic. I don't know how my ancestors let themselves be driven underground by you humans.'

'So, this act. It was just for another laugh? Is that all you do, toy with us? Does that really make you any more grown up than me? Any different? How old are you anyway?'

'Oh Maxy, I thought it was impolite for humans to ask such things?' Lucky looked at Max laying on the floor with no emotion on her ageless face. 'I am tremendously different. I have seen how you all live, the animals have shown me. I play with you because it serves me to see your repeated pain. It does not cost me. It fills me with hope that someday soon, you will destroy yourselves and we will claim the land back.'

'We? There's no one here but you. This place is barren. You're scared, you're hiding down here. Why not come out if you're so tremendous?'

'Come now,' she said, turning away and getting back to whatever she was doing before. 'I'm not a fish to be baited onto such a thin line. We shall travel to The Dark One and then you shall see our numbers.'

'Ballshit—' Once again, Max felt the effect of the strike but not the impact. How did she close the distance so quickly? His head was snapped backwards and his limp body followed as he crashed down on his back. The shotgun went flying into the air, flapping its two halves like a shot bird and as luck would have it, the stock landed square on his crotch. He huffed as the dull pain flared and realised he had now just regained feeling there. He rolled onto his side, into the foetal position.

'Blasphemy,' she repeated and went back to her work.

Max decided that The Dark One most likely did exist and they would in fact be going on some journey after all. He looked across the floor to Enid who had been watching this with silent tears rolling down her face. She sucked vigorously on her hands and Max feared that before long she might lose her mind in all this madness. But then perhaps she didn't have too long left anyway? He tried to push the thought away, but it had become a crushing weight he could no longer breathe through. They were both doomed.

'I'm sorry,' he said, now crying with her. 'I'm so sorry darling—' Here he was once more, bested by Lucky and down for the count. He might as well shit himself again and bring it full circle. He let the throbbing pain in his crotch dissipate but he stayed down. He felt like he had been thrown back in time and was no more than a smeared mirror of Enid right now. Where she had a runny nose, his was bloodied; where she was fresh out the womb, he wanted to crawl back in. They both knew their fate. All he wanted to do was hold her until Lucky was done with him. There was no point in rushing Lucky physically and trying to overwhelm her; he had tasted her supernatural speed. Max was finally able to sit up. Lucky was paying him no attention, but why would she? The shotgun lay beside him as useless as the poker he had used in the forest.

'When?' he simply asked. She slowly turned, satisfaction glowing on that eternal face.

'It's good to see you are finally coming to terms with the situation. It will be easier for us all if you do. We will leave when I am ready.'

Max thought about asking when exactly that was but didn't want to know how much time they had left. He opened his arms to Enid but she shook her head. He tried again and added a little flap of his fingers.

She came. They hugged briefly while she stood and then Max picked her up and put her on his lap. *What the—*

## 38

Was this another trick? Max adjusted Enid on his lap to make sure.

*Nope.*

The spare cartridge – his last cartridge – was still in his pocket, packed full of salt and ready to rock. Or had Lucky slipped this out and stuffed it with silly-string for one last prank? Max was about to find out and he didn't mean to waste a second. He planted a kiss on Enid's head then lifted her off his lap and put her to the side.

She protested but he gave her a stern hush. Lucky chuckled.

'Good. Show me you're worth keeping around,' she said, still looking away. Would it really be this easy? After all the times he had been fooled by this ancient monster, was their salvation really mistaken in his pocket like some meagre manhood? Was she prudish? He found it peculiar now that she had thrown a robe on to cover herself after such a display in the woods, and in his dreams. Perhaps she really *was* too prudish to have checked his pockets.

Max took a breath to make sure he didn't faint. He dug into the pocket and felt the plastic cartridge with its brass base – it sure felt like the same one he put in there. The shotgun lay beside him already broken. He casually pulled out the cartridge and slid it into the left barrel; it entered smoothly. Max lifted the gun quickly, placed the barrel between his two big toes so it pointed straight at Lucky's back and snapped it shut.

Lucky turned with no look of concern on her face. Just as one looks at a creaking tree in the wind. I wonder if my feet are working yet, Max thought?

He gave his toes a wiggle, they waved back.

He pulled the trigger.

The wind was instantly knocked out of him. This time there was recoil and there was screaming. Real, guttural screaming, and it was coming from Lucky. Max looked to Enid and she had both her sodden hands over her ears with her cherub face scrunched. He wasn't sure if it was the ringing in his own ears or the screaming from Lucky, but he simply grinned at his daughter.

God, he loved her.

Lucky had just made it to Max's feet. She had moved with that rapid speed once again but had been caught in the snare of the blast.

Max got up and felt a flaring pain in his gut that made him stumble. It turned out there *were* worse pains than getting hit in the balls. He casually wondered if he might have ruptured something where the stock had recoiled into his stomach, but he'd address that later. He found his feet and stood over Lucky.

She was writhing like a paper bag in a tornado. The sight was horrifying. Parts of her face contorted through various emotions independently, as the embers took hold. Her eyes were in shock while her mouth grimaced in pain. Age seemed to finally catch up with her immortal form, and she was not ageing well. Her thrashing clubbed the floor harder and harder. The hut began to shake and Enid screamed.

Without thinking of the consequences, Max quickly grabbed Lucky by her wild hair and dragged her towards the side room, away from Enid. It turned out Lucky was light as a feather.

Her screams doubled as her body convulsed. Her hands flew around at an unnatural speed and caught Max's forearms where pain promptly seared, but he held on tight. She was out of control; she was *suffering*.

He tossed her the remaining distance into the little room she had been busying herself in. His arm bled heavily. Max knew he should grab Enid and leave, but he couldn't pull himself away. He was sure he'd be haunted by the nightmare of this dying tyrant in years to come but he *had* to stay. Max waited until the screaming ceased and the racing embers had completely engulfed Lucky's body and robe, leaving behind a glowing coal figure in her place.

It was… beautiful.

Max approached. Somewhere behind him a child was screaming. Max was now in the side room. Fragments began to sizzle then fell off the petrified figure, from the extremities inwards – fingers and toes, forearms and shins, until just the torso and head remained.

He heard more screams from behind, staccato as they fought for air.

Then the head fell off and sizzled into the root

covered ground which caught fire. He should probably leave now, but there was something, something... else to do. Max blinked as the torso finally gave way with a sigh. Lucky's final breath. These also caught on the ground. *Now* he should really leave before the whole place went up. But then he saw it. The flames were dancing around something that had just been revealed in the heart of the torso. Well, it might even *be* Lucky's heart.

A crystal.

No bigger than a fist and cut in asymmetrical lines which made it look as if it was moving among the flames, *pulsing*. Was it over now? Before he could consider it further, he reached down and snatched it from the wreckage as if someone else might take it first. It felt warm in his hand for a moment and then the heat dissipated, and with it any thoughts of importance or wonder. He popped it in his pocket as if he'd just found a penny on the floor.

Enid's screams stopped.

He stood over the carbon carcass and exhaled. Now it was done, his head cleared in an instant. The madness of the situation, the calamity of the trip, the guilt for his sister. It was gone.

*Enid!*

Max spun around to find Enid sitting quietly in the room behind, her face was streaked with tears and snot. He ran over and quickly scooped her up.

She gave him a brief look of disdain for his absence but then buried her head into his neck in relief.

Max turned for one last look at what remained of Lucky and was greeted with an entire room in flames.

That'll do it, he thought, then headed out into the purple twilight.

The clean air made him realise what a putrid smell he'd been breathing in while he watched Lucky die. It was sulphuric and old. Behind him, the crackling of fire grew as Lucky's hut went up in flames lighting their way home.

Enid stirred as they reached the inverted fields and after some comforting she started nattering happily as they went, just as if she'd woken from a bad dream.

*Ah, to be so young and distracted.*

Speaking of distractions, now with Enid safely in his arms, he looked around and tried to take in more of this magical world. There wasn't much more to learn in the valley of this inverted village, but the stars above burned with an intensity he'd never seen before. The usual culprits of Sirius and Canopus stung his eyes, yet they didn't distract from the beauty of the remaining canopy. The great arch of the Milky Way slashed through the sky in such clarity it looked close enough to touch. Thoughts of Carla came to the front of his mind. He looked around to orientate himself as she had taught him all those years ago and was greeted by the Big Dipper. He followed the tip of the pan across and his eyes came to rest on Polaris, the North Star.

'Incredible,' he said aloud. They were on an inverted plane yet the skies were the same.

He didn't have trouble finding the hawthorn again. As he approached the forest, it was clear to see its root tips swaying high above the rest as they twinkled in the starlight. Max entered the forest watching his steps as he went – not wanting to crunch anything. Although Max thought he loved nature already, the sight of these living roots had given him a deep empathy for the plants and trees he had never felt before. They really were alive, and humans, were really fucking it all up. Lucky had that much right.

He felt the crystal jostle in his pocket as he walked.

As he passed the swaying roots he reached out and stroked their tender flesh, they responded to his touch but did not try to grab or strangle. They softly weaved around his hand like a cat's tail and the friction sent off little sparks which didn't fade but rose slowly like fireflies. Enid watched them go up and clapped.

The crystal hummed for the briefest of moments then fell silent.

# ACKNOWLEDGMENTS

A big thank you to Dave for giving this the once over and clearly pointing out that everyone should be drinking stout. As always, shout out to Mike for the beautiful cover art.

Most importantly, I'd like to acknowledge you, the reader. Thank you so much for reading, I really do hope you enjoyed it. If you have a moment, please do leave a review on the book's Amazon page. If you liked this book, you'll most likely enjoy my others as well. Go on, treat yourself.

# ABOUT THE AUTHOR

Massimo Paradiso is a short-form producer, loud drummer and the author of three novels. Each have staggeringly sold at least one copy. He lives in Sussex with his wife and daughter.

massimoparadiso.com

Printed in Great Britain
by Amazon